T0103466

A LIFETIME'S
WORTH

A LIFETIME'S WORTH

Anuja Siraj

PARTRIDGE
A Penguin Random House Company

Copyright © 2015 by Anuja Siraj.

ISBN: Softcover   978-1-4828-4951-6
                eBook   978-1-4828-4952-3

All rights reserved. No part of this book may be used or reproduced by any means, graphic, electronic, or mechanical, including photocopying, recording, taping or by any information storage retrieval system without the written permission of the publisher except in the case of brief quotations embodied in critical articles and reviews.

Because of the dynamic nature of the Internet, any web addresses or links contained in this book may have changed since publication and may no longer be valid. The views expressed in this work are solely those of the author and do not necessarily reflect the views of the publisher, and the publisher hereby disclaims any responsibility for them.

This is a work of fiction. All of the characters, names, incidents, organizations, and dialogue in this novel are either the products of the author's imagination or are used fictitiously.

Print information available on the last page.

To order additional copies of this book, contact
Partridge India
000 800 10062 62
orders.india@partridgepublishing.com

www.partridgepublishing.com/india

TITLES

TITLES

INTRODUCTION

What you are about to embark upon in this book is, in the words of the young author, "a collection of sixteen stories with ordinary characters whose experiences reflect the reality of the world around us."

And what a world it is, providing a glimpse into a palimpsest of existences of the kind that we might have known through conversations, stories told to us, movies, television serials, and of course through books!

Let me explain what I mean. Anuja's stories are about human experiences, but most of them come to us through the prism of Western culture and that is what makes them interesting. These are stories about joy, sadness, loneliness, generosity, childishness, maturity, weakness and strength, the loss of and the discovery of identity, all of which always make for good stories, if not always gripping ones. Anuja's, however, presumably born from her own experience of a life lived largely abroad, focus on specific experiences and situations, and though her strokes tend to be very broad, she sustains reader interest by a pacey style and great use of language.

What is astounding is that these stories, some of them surprisingly adult in the gaze they turn on the characters that people them, were written when she was between the ages of 11 and 14. They weave tales around very specific situations that touch human lives. Anuja's pivots are the basic human emotions – a bit of joy, plenty of sadness, pathos, loneliness, fear, uncertainty and even despair, but she is well aware that of these human emotions, in all their permutations and combinations, the world's stories are made. She also knows that custom doesn't stale the infinite variety of the human experience, and that no matter how often you may have entered a story pivoted upon a particular set of circumstances, handling and style and the personal impact of the writer can make all things new.

It is important to understand all this, for right now, the author is at the start of her game. This is a curve that is at the beginning of its journey into a life of writing. I am sure readers will find much to enjoy here, and more to which to look forward.

Carol Andrade

[Carol Andrade has had a career in journalism spanning over four decades and has worked for the Times of India, Midday and Afternoon DC, holding various positions. She was the first female reporter of the Times of India. She is currently the Dean at St. Paul's Institute of Communication Education, Mumbai, India.]

AUTHOR'S NOTE

When I decided to bring out this book, I didn't have to search too hard for a title. 'A Lifetime's Worth' just sounded right because that's exactly what this is.

These characters are ordinary people who needed their stories told, and even though it wasn't deliberate, I realize now that what happens to each of them reflects reality in more ways that I can describe. Some of them are inspired by real people and conversations. Sixteen selected short tales written by yours truly from the age of eleven are brought together in this book to celebrate a little over a decade of storytelling- the adventure I call my life.

Now for gratitude; I am overwhelmed. Praise to Almighty God for all His bounty and guidance, which continues to define me. Many thanks to my family for putting up with my insanity while I stay holed up to write! Gosh, do I annoy you guys! Also, thanks to my illustrator- who is also my first reader and my sister.

I'm grateful to my editors and illustrators at the now defunct imprint of the Dubai-based Khaleej Times, known as The Young Times. You were the beginning and you are remembered today. I also thank the editorial team at The Teenager Today for continued support through the years. Thank you to Ms. Carol Andrade for the pride and honor of such a lovely introduction to this book. Much love to the teachers who believed in me, and the friends who never left my side.

When this book is read, a child's dream comes true. The dream to be able to tell stories to a world that listens. Thank you for listening.

Delighted,
Anuja Siraj

For My Family

PART I

Right Here, Right Now

1. THE BROWN DOVE'S NEST

Kayla sat on the floor, pressing her face against the French window. On the other side of it, there was a ledge with railings, and on that ledge sat a brown dove. About eight months ago, Kayla's mother had filled a plastic bowl with water and placed it on the ledge for birds. In the dusty city, birds could get thirsty very often. Kayla had been really excited and ran to the French window in her room every day after school to watch for birds, hoping they would come drink water from the bowl.

Now the sun had dried up all the water and the wind had tipped the bowl onto its side and blown it to the end of the ledge. It was stuck there between the window and the rails, and that's where the brown dove sat. Kayla had noticed the bird before. It would come and peck around the same spot where the bowl sat on its side, and then go away. Hours later, the brown dove would come again. Kayla had known something was going to happen.

The next day when Kayla came home, the brown dove was sitting inside the bowl. Another brown dove flew up to the ledge and brought it a twig. A few minutes later, another twig appeared. Kayla's eyes lit up; the brown doves were building a nest.

Kayla's mother, Adriana was doing the dishes in the kitchen. Adriana was angrier than usual today. Hector, Kayla's father, sat at his laptop computer, tapping away. Hector's phone rang frequently; it was work, he said. Kayla believed him, but Adriana believed no one. For as long as Kayla could remember, her parents had fought. They disliked each other immensely and sometimes Kayla wondered until her little head hurt, what two people could do to each other that would make them despise each other so intensely.

It had all begun with Adriana's childhood, or at least that's what she claimed to her therapist. Adriana hated her sister and most of the people in her life. She distrusted her mother. She feared her neighbors. She was disgusted by Hector. She was oblivious to her daughter. Adriana had taken psychiatric drugs for most of her marital life. She had once tried to convince Kayla that she would need the same drugs someday too. Kayla was ten.

The brown dove was bringing more twigs to Kayla's window. She watched with amazement, at how the male just kept coming back, never once forgetting the way, never once lost or lazy. The female kept moving around in the plastic bowl that was stuck on its side, and Kayla realized it was trying to see if a nest could survive in the bowl. Kayla ran home from school to sit on the floor and watch the brown doves build their home every day. The twigs kept falling off the ledge when the female turned around in the bowl.

Every day, all the twigs fell off, and the male simply brought more. It just wasn't happening, but the birds kept at it. Kayla realized she had to do something, but she knew that the birds would be spooked if she tried to help. Despite that, she rummaged around the apartment and found some thread and scrunched up tissues. Then she opened the French window and dropped them onto the ledge when the birds weren't there.

Adriana was unpleasant, more so each day. Hector had been transferred to his construction company's new branch and was tired of driving all the way to work. He tried never to show it, but the lines creasing his forehead told Kayla that he was anxious and unhappy. Kayla worried about her dad. During the day when Hector was away and Adriana was quieter, Kayla obsessed with the brown dove that sat in the bowl on the ledge outside her window. On the weekends when Hector was home, Kayla watched the brown doves in fascination while her parents bickered incessantly in the background, forgetting the child that sat quietly on the floor.

Kayla crossed her little fingers, hoping the bird would notice the dirty old thread and the crumpled tissue, but it did not. Instead, the male brought another twig, and surprisingly, a paper clip. The female quickly pushed the twigs and the paper clip under her body and nestled onto the collection. Kayla watched, astonished, as the male brought another paper clip from somewhere. *Maybe he went into a stationery store*, she thought excitedly. *Or the curb in front of a stationery store,* she decided after some thought. He was a bird, after all.

The male brought twigs and paper clips, the wind blew most of it away, but the birds were persistent. Sometimes the male pressed his chest against the female's head and would stay still for a few seconds before he left for twigs. Occasionally a mynah dropped by, snooping around to break into an egg and feed, but the male dove drove it away. It was truly remarkable.

When the twigs kept falling off the ledge, Kayla was disappointed and worried that the birds would leave. She craned her neck to see; the dove had laid no eggs yet, perhaps because the nest kept falling apart no matter how many times the birds pushed the twigs together. In the background, Adriana screamed at Hector almost on a daily basis, and refused to take her medicines. The nesting brown dove's frequent cooing upset her, and she cursed at it. Kayla did not like that at all.

The weather forecasting man in the TV said that there was going to be a horrible storm that night, and maybe the birds cooed because they sensed that a storm was coming. The TV man also said that schools in the city would be closed the next few days.

That night the storm came, but Kayla heard noises over the howling of the wind and the rain. She clambered out of bed to go find her parents. She saw that Hector and Adriana were in a horrible fight, and Adriana was almost strangling him. There were bruise marks on Hector's arms and chest, and his face bled where Adriana's nails had dug into his skin. Kayla held her hand over her own mouth, frightened and in tears.

She watched Adriana push Hector against the wall screaming in a voice completely unlike that of the mother that she loved so much. Out of the corner of his eyes, Hector suddenly saw that Kayla was awake and at the bedroom door. Hector's eyes widened and ever so slightly, he shook his head at Kayla while trying in vain to hold Adriana away- it broke the child's heart.

Silently, Kayla went into her room and climbed back into bed. She lay curled up under her blanket shivering and sobbed until she fell asleep.

The next morning Hector went to work with a gash under his eyes. Adriana wanted to leave without a good bye. She packed her bags and pulled Kayla away from the French window. Kayla cried and struggled against her mother's vice-like grip in vain. Sobbing uncontrollably, she turned one last time to look at the ledge outside the French window.

Rain had lashed at the ledge all night, and the last remaining twigs lay broken and wet near the plastic bowl that was perched on its side. The birds were gone. The storm had destroyed the brown dove's nest, but theirs hadn't been the only home lost.

THE END

2. MIDLIFE CRISIS

Every day as he walked down the same street and went back home, he'd wonder the same thing. Was this it? He would look at all the other people around him, going about their lives and he would want to scream out in frustration. Did they not notice? Did they not worry? Well of course they did; they noticed their deadlines and worried about their bills.

But was that all? Come on... was there nothing more to this life than, oh, school through college, then the rejections on the job hunt, then the mounting stress levels of a job if in fact it is obtained, all the way to bills and family and, well. More worries. The cycle that his family were in. The one that these other people were in. Shudder.

At family meetings, people said that he looked too sad for his age. He was too 'droopy', they said. He did look around curiously to see what he was meant to look like. Plenty of subjects were around. He saw and he knew what they were trying to tell him but somehow, it wasn't in his control. It wasn't that he was sad, it was more...melancholy. For no apparent reason. He had reason, but they would never understand. They'd just shake their heads and get on with their insane race to nowhere in particular.

At night he'd lay awake for hours, and everyone actually thought that was ordinary. When the neighbor kids called him to play, he'd decline with a blank face. No one understood the turmoil within his little soul, no one imagined that he worried for the world's future. Oh, how hostile a place it was!

The truth was that, at an age so young, he was barely anywhere to be calling it a crisis. He just heard things, saw things and felt deeply conflicted on a thousand different levels. He had only just stopped being a child and yet he felt ancient inside, and completely, utterly powerless every minute of every day.

If he ever actually admitted to feeling this way, they would never take him seriously. They would say that people go through this all the time at some point in their lives and that it was going to be okay.

Well, people were sometimes morons. And in a world full of them morons, an English bulldog's gotta be smarter than that, he thought, shaking his head. Then he went back to licking his bowl clean.

THE END

3. THE NEXT BEST THING

"**I** believe in destiny. I believe that things do happen for a reason. Even if that's just bollocks, the faith does help- it sort of keeps me going. Also, my parents didn't really give me much choice, did they, now? My name is Destiny Marie Myers, and it's a pleasure to make your acquaintance."

The doctor smiled nonchalantly and shook the girl's hand briefly before going back to the medical chart on her clipboard. I thought that was a bit rude; she could have introduced herself too or at least said something. The girl seemed nice. Being a man I noticed that she definitely *looked* nice too.

The doctor studied the chart and nodded at the patient, indicating that everything looked fine. She then turned to leave the room and I followed promptly. "So, uh, Daniel," she said to me, now poring over some other patient's test result of some sort as she walked briskly while I almost jogged to keep up. "We don't talk to a lot of pharmaceutical reps other than our regulars."

She slowed down- we had reached her office- and I narrowly avoided colliding with a couple of nurses. I will never admit to it but I was a bit breathless trying to keep up with this woman. "I'll only be a few minutes, Dr. Lloyd," I told her earnestly. She stepped into her office and looked slightly impatient but not unpleasant. "I believe you, but I'm busy the rest of the day. Come by tomorrow; can you do that?" She said, looking amused but not unkindly.

"Absolutely! Of course I can do that! Thanks so much Dr. Lloyd!" She had already moved onto a phone call, dismissing me with a wave.

* *

The next day I was there on time as promised, to give Dr. Lloyd the presentation I had worked really hard on. I was new to the job so I had had a lot of studying to do for this presentation. All my boss would tell me was that I was to be able to sell the drug to anyone- even to an angry bear that wanted to rip my head off. He said that's what a good rep could do. I was terrified- I did not think I could sell much to a bear under any circumstance. My boss's examples did not tend to be of much help.

Dr. Lloyd was inside a patient's room with her clipboard so I waited outside. When I casually glanced into the room I noticed that this was the same patient I'd seen her with the day before. I couldn't hear what was being said, but Dr. Lloyd briefly shook the woman's hand again before examining her. I was distracted when a bickering couple walked right past me and I began to wonder why such good looking wives had to be this difficult, especially considering the husband's pained expression.

A couple of minutes later the doctor stepped out and nodded at me- I had called her that morning just to make sure she could see me. I followed her nervously into her office to pitch the company's new drug.

When I was done, she stood up immediately, glancing at her watch. "Alright then, Daniel," she spoke while walking to the door. The meeting was obviously over, so I gathered all my material and followed suit. Not a lot of people could really look good in scrubs but Dr. Lloyd was pulling it off, I noticed, despite my worry about the outcome of the meeting.

"We'll take it, but email the proposal to the ID's that I gave you and uh, cc me, will you. I won't remember all of that," she joked. I could breathe again! I had done well!

Dr. Lloyd had already begun walking while I stood basking in my glory so I knew I had better run if I wanted to thank her. "You've been kind to me doctor, contrary to what I'd thought," I blurted out.

She raised her eyebrows. "What *did* you think?" She looked pleasantly curious. I wondered if I was going to jeopardize my hard earned opportunity with the unnecessary truth.

"Erm… well… it's nothing. It's just, that patient that you were with today when I got here…"

"Yeah. What about her?"

"It's nothing really… but earlier when she introduced herself to you… she seemed really nice… you know…I mean…"

I was kind of worried now and cursed myself for not having kept my mouth shut. The doctor was slowing down. "You didn't really respond to her. So I thought maybe…" God, what had I done? I had basically just called her incredibly rude- now she would not recommend MedCorp's drug and my huge mouth will have destroyed my commission and quite possibly my job.

Dr. Lloyd did not look too pleasant anymore and there was that air of nonchalance again. "Come with me," she said, and I followed her to what I realized was the room of the woman that I had just mentioned, having successfully annoyed the one good doctor who hadn't been a snob to me this past week.

I stepped inside behind the doctor and watched her smile down at the patient. This girl was really pretty, I observed again despite the sad predicament I had dragged myself into. She smiled back at the doctor and spoke.

"I believe in destiny." The girl told the doctor earnestly. "I believe that things do happen for a reason. Even if that's just bollocks, the faith does help- it sort of keeps me going. Also, my parents didn't really give me much choice, did they, now?" she smiled again, and my heart suddenly just felt really cold.

"My name is Destiny Marie Myers, and it's a pleasure to make your acquaintance." She held her hand out once again, and Dr. Lloyd took it patiently, once again, and shook it gently without hurting her where it was hooked to the IV.

Then the doctor led me back outside and closed the door behind her. I did not have the slightest idea what to say. Dr. Lloyd began walking, and I did too, turning one last time to catch a glimpse of Destiny Marie Myers.

"Post traumatic amnesia. She was raped and beaten to an inch of her life. Her brain is protecting her from the memory. You're right- she *is* a nice kid," the doctor added.

I was silent.

"She's already been through neuro. I'm still taking care of the rest. Her family says they're glad, in a way, that she can't remember any of what happened to her. They say that Destiny is such a soft and unassuming girl that she would have wanted death if she could remember what she's been through."

Walking back through the hospital gates and out into the sun-lit parking lot, I couldn't really take my mind off what I'd heard. Destiny's words kept echoing in my thoughts and every time, that vision of her holding her hand out just kept returning to me. I realized that every day Dr. Lloyd would listen as Destiny introduced herself over and over again, assuming they'd never met. I could never imagine the horror that Destiny had endured, but I realized what it meant if her own parents were grateful that her memories had been erased.

They knew her the best… so they say that she would have been so traumatized that she would have chosen death over the pain. I realized that even though she would have wanted an end, what she got was, in a way, a beginning. She'd tell Dr. Lloyd the same things every day until one day when the injuries disappeared; then she could begin a life where there was no remnant of the past.

I'd never known Destiny Marie Myers, but somehow I felt that if she ever knew, she would say that no, this hadn't been the easier end… but that this had, indeed, been the next best thing.

THE END

4. TREVOR'S MOTHER

Ever watched the break of dawn? The actual moment when the first ray of light touches darkness, when birdsong ends the silence that lasted through the night? Then the sun comes up, and it's warm and wonderful again. So many sounds together, it's like listening to the heart beat of a huge harmony that we somehow dance to unknowingly. It's beautiful, that moment of realization, when we finally convince ourselves, that all of hope isn't gone.

I remember when Trevor was born. He had a surrogate mother and then, well, me. I was there when he came, and his mother was an 18 year old girl who badly needed the money for a reason she never told us. But she was desperate and so were we. She left very quickly and didn't stay to meet her son.

I remember holding him, and his little fingers wrapped around my wedding ring and I thought that maybe, just maybe, it was time for me to finally feel that happiness; to fill that empty space in my life.

The feeling of bringing a little person into the world is like daybreak. It is the faint warmth that streak of light brings when you're plunging headlong into darkness, when you're blinded with pain, and when you know you're on your own. It is when you look at those people around you; those wonderful people who make you want to pull through somehow.

When the pain is at its worst, when you can't feel your own body anymore, and you listen to your own voice screaming in anguish and it's ringing in your ears until you want it all to end. And then... somehow, all it takes, is another voice, blending into yours, a little battle cry, of joy, of triumph, saying hey world, I'm here.

Funny how then your senses are instantly protective, and with the last bit of strength left in your exhausted frame, all you need to know is that there's a little person right there, the priceless face you have dreamed of seeing for a very long time, the voice you longed to hear, the fingers you wanted to feel for real, the fragile little thing that somehow just came from inside of you. That's like a burst of birdsong in daybreak, and that's like hope incessantly fighting against despair. That's magic, right there.

I've never known any of this. I have never felt that pain worse than bones being broken together or limbs being torn, and I have never felt the joy of knowing you created something more beautiful than the entire universe put together. But I have been a mother, and I have loved. That day when I held the little boy in my arms, I felt light-headed with happiness, and I promised myself that I would give him everything I could.

I would do everything a mother did, and in the end all that mattered was that I had him, and it was me who was holding him close now, and it was my face that he would remember as his mother's. It was me that he would call 'mum', and that was all that mattered.

"Sheriff, I have 181 coming in, homicide on 23rd Becker's west," the walkie- talkie crackled to life on my belt and I snatched it up without blinking. Years of being a cop does that to you. When bad things happen, you're not surprised anymore. "Calling in emergency, 181 needs back-up on 23rd Becker's west," I barked into it and got into my car.

Outside, it was a perfectly normal morning, and the world was going on as it did on every other ordinary day. A breeze was rustling the ends of my hair where I had snipped it short many years ago, almost like the feeling of an amputated limb. I let my fingers run through my hair and concentrated on what was coming. I don't miss my long hair. It has been gone for too long now.

What I did miss, though, was the element of being surprised in life. I have reached this point of time when nothing can startle me, nothing can frighten me. I'm just too prepared for ambush, to strike back, to defend, to kick asses. I'm just too vigilant all the time that it's like I have been everywhere and seen everything in the world. There's nothing out there that can make me cry too hard or laugh too loud. I'm controlled, composed and ready for anything, at any time. Life fights to take me by surprise now.

"You should really take that vacation, the one you've been postponing you know, Sheriff," my deputy tells me. "Are you calling me a workaholic again, Robert," I raised my eyebrows, and Robert immediately looked apologetic. "I'm not one, you know," I corrected him. "I just am too good at what I do," I chuckled, more to myself. Robert smiled, and nodded ahead. We were at the site of the homicide. I got out slowly and my walkie-talkie crackled again. "181, calling in for back-up—"

"Oh give it a rest already, Isaac, we're here now," I said callously kicking a stone aside and strolling into the crime scene with my hands in my pocket. Isaac turned at my voice. "Morning, Sheriff." I answered with one-tenth of a nod and strode on. I could have been in a garden, the way I moved. Seriously, I'm not heartless. I'm just so used to everything bad in the world and I'm just, you know, passive.

Cops were walking around and an ambulance with a blaring siren parked itself haphazardly beside another police car with only Isaac that had been here before us. "Victims found on the floor, bleeding from head-wound, and multiple wounds, one male and one female..." Isaac was reading off his records and all I heard was blah. "Sure, sure," I muttered, kicking aside a ball idly and lifting the bright yellow tape that had 'CRIME SCENE DO NOT ENTER' stamped all over it.

"How long?" I asked. "Not long, Sheriff. We got here minutes back and you were fast." Isaac replied. "Of course I was. Both dead when you boys get here?" Isaac nodded.

I saw the man first as my eyes scanned the room, zooming in on the bottles stashed behind the trash can, the one at his feet, half of its contents in a pool by his side. Cheap beer. He would be roughly five foot nine, around forty five years of miserable life, it would have been a drug OD if not this reason for him to die. Typical. I, of course, didn't give a shit.

Then I saw the woman. I saw her face, and my eyes zeroed in on her eyelashes. They were moving. I froze when I saw who she was, and years down the memory lane flashed back to those moments when this face had been in my life. "MEDIC!" I barked, crouching at her side, holding her hand. "Over here, this one has a pulse, OVER HERE!" I yelled orders, and soon my deputies had her aided and bound to a stretcher and packed into the ambulance.

For the first time in so many years, I had been taken by surprise, and I had forgotten who I was for a moment when those memories came back. I knew her. I knew that woman. I just didn't want to know her. I hadn't ever wanted to meet her again. But then I did, and the super-cop I prided myself on being just ceased to exist for that split-second when I was just, well, me. Trevor's mum.

"How's she holding on?" I asked, not stopping for Robert to match my pace as I strode into the hospital. "Barely," he replied, walking fast beside me. "Some guys from her, uh boyfriend's circle. Drugs and gambling and all of that. Got into a fight. She just got in between and took a bad blow to the base of her skull. Neighbors heard them. Called in quick. That's the story." I nodded, slowing down as we approached Accident and Trauma Care. "Get me what you have on the woman," I told him, and Robert nodded and left.

The doctor told me pretty much the same thing in medical terms, and I knew she was slipping. She was hemorrhaging. I wasn't sure it was the same person, maybe I'd made a mistake. I should be glad I'd saved someone's life, again. Not this weird feeling I had, like she'd come to get Trevor or something. This weird stupid mother thing. I'm the cop, here, for crying out loud.

"Sheriff, she's conscious now, I think you should come in. The bleeding has been controlled; it's the OD in her blood that's a problem. And Sheriff, she's lost a lot of blood, so I'd appreciate if you kept most of the questions for later," the doctor told me. I nodded and rubbed my index finger against the permanent frown between my eyebrows as if to straighten it, and nodded at the doctor.

I went in that door a person, and I know I walked out of there as someone else.

She looked at me, her one eye swollen and half-open. Her other eye shone a lovely blue. I'd never forgotten those eyes. I knew it really was her. "I don't believe you remember me, officer," she croaked, and instinctively I turned on my heels and looked for some water. When she had gulped it down, she lay back again, and I saw how frail she looked. Still so young and pretty.

"Who did this to you?" was my first question, even though what I really wanted to say was something between 'you want Trevor back, don't you?' and 'back off and leave my son alone before I put a bullet through your head'.

But I couldn't bring myself to threaten her. I just held my head down, barely able to look at her. I felt like I'd done something wrong, like I was the criminal now. Like I was afraid of this little woman lying on a hospital bed with not a single person in the world to bring her a bouquet of flowers or a balloon to tell her that if something happened to her it would matter.

I felt stupid. I felt mean. I felt angry at myself for wanting to threaten her, for wanting her to go away. And above all of that, I felt frightened by the idea of this woman coming back into my life claiming what was indeed hers, in a way.

"You know the story, Sheriff," she said, sounding slightly better. "My life is like that. Always has been. I knew it would come to this someday."

"Then you should stop being like this," I heard myself saying.

"I can't," she whispered. "It's who I am. It would take courage to change that."

I looked away, my lips trembling. I wasn't a cop anymore, and I was certainly not tough. I was afraid because of the bad mum I had been to Trevor, because Robert had been right when he asked me to stop working all the time, because of what I felt when every night my husband added another box to the pile of moldy take-out boxes of Chinese and Indian that cluttered the otherwise unmarred serenity of my kitchen and went to bed silently, because of the emptiness I felt for myself when I drank one mug of coffee after another during my all-nighters and dabbed at the tears in my eyes that would never come.

"You have to be brave then," I blurted out. "We all do." I watched her sigh. "I don't have a home to go to. I don't have a place in the world I can fit into, and I don't have anything to be brave for anymore." She let out a small sob.

My head was aching again, that familiar feeling when I wanted to cry but I just couldn't. My lachrymal glands have been this stubborn for as long as I remember, by the way. I don't cry. "That's not true," I heard myself say. I grit my teeth. She gazed up at me, her blue eyes blinking. I felt stupid. I had no earthly idea what I was doing. "You should meet Trevor."

She blinked blankly, and with crushing force I realized that she wasn't...well. Trevor wasn't her only child. She had done that for money more than once. "Uhm," I faltered, wondering what to say. "I mean, you should come home. Meet Trev. He's your son." When I said that, the corners of her bright blue eyes crinkled into a kind smile, and I looked away. "*Your* son, Sheriff. He's *your* son."

* *

"You're afraid of me," she told me the next day, her expression unreadable. I pushed her food tray closer to her and watched the nurse fluff her pillows and nod at her blood bag and leave. "Why would you say that?" I put on a brilliant smile, shaking my head. "I've had people die at my hands. I've been stabbed. I've been threatened multiple times. I deliver a very nice punch. Takes a lot, you know, to frighten me," I laughed, expecting her to be awed like everyone else.

"You're afraid," she repeated. I frowned slightly now, and uncovered the glass of orange juice and held it out to her. She took it. "I know fear when I see it, Sheriff. I know that you've been through a lifetime of ensuring that things don't go wrong. For other people." I looked away.

"You see that's the problem," she continued. "You're too tough. You're too ready for... for anything. You can't be surprised. You're worried you haven't been a good mother." I looked up sharply. "I'm not sure I want to have this conversation, Hailey," I said icily. "I haven't mentioned I have any problems or that I require help of any kind."

"You don't need to. I can see it. You should know you can talk to me, sheriff. Woman to woman," she grinned, and her stitches probably hurt because she flinched. But I could see that her blue eyes were bright with kindness and curiosity. I didn't trust her. I didn't trust anybody on the face of the planet. I only trusted my instincts and I acted according to them. "You don't trust me," she whispered, and it was my turn to flinch. I was pretty sure I hadn't said a word out loud, but she seemed to know.

"Its fine, you know. You don't have to be so tough on yourself. You can be super-cop part-time," she chuckled, flinching again. She coughed, and I held out the juice which she waved away. "And the rest of the time, you can be what you want to be. What you've always wanted to be. Trevor's mum." I stared outside the window, not wanting to look at her. I was surprised mildly, the way she was reading straight off my thoughts. I didn't want to accept it.

"You don't know anything," I heard myself say. "It takes strength to ask for help," she responded calmly. "It means a lot to protect the lives of people, to have them die in your hands. It affects you. It changes something inside of you. And in as many years as you have been doing that, it makes you tough. But," she coughed again, and heaved. "Drink up, hush," I said, coaxing her to have some water. She did, and lay back.

I couldn't believe I was listening to this woman I barely knew and I couldn't believe I actually cared. "But it takes even more," she continued, "to have people live at your hands, as in, to have them depend on you for the little things in life. To have a person grow up before you. To watch him become all the things you want him to be. All before your eyes. To have a family to call your own."

I thought of the time I'd caught Trev smoking, to all the dinners we never sat together and had, to all the school events I could never make it to, to all the nights I spend awake. To the town I'd lay my life down to protect, but the little boy I'd left vulnerable meanwhile. My son.

"It's alright to be afraid," Hailey whispered, her hands closing over mine.

"It's scary huh," I nodded, more to myself. I could never share anything with anybody. I've never cried for as long as time and I don't count on anything except my department to help out. I don't ask for help. And yet here I was. "It's scary, with everything that goes on around a kid these days, and I, well. I haven't really been there for him," it came out as a whisper, and I held my head down. "Scary, quite," Hailey agreed, patting my hand softly. "You can make it right, though. There's time."

"There is?"

"There is."

"Come home," I blurted out. "Don't leave when you're out of here. Meet Trev. Talk to him."

"Sheriff," she smiled, shaking her head, watching me with twinkling eyes. "I said there's time for *you*."

Then Hailey began coughing, and this time she didn't stop. She was struggling and instinctively I jammed my finger into the emergency button beside her bed and it wailed for about a minute before a nurse came rushing in, followed by another one, who waved for me to get out. I kept glancing at Hailey convulsing and coughing as I rushed out of the nurses' way, and I walked out of the hospital, right outside into the lounge where I had a coffee from the vending machine. I cracked my knuckles and stretched myself, forcing something inside to subside. I glanced at the watch from habit more than necessity.

"Doctor," I called, walking over to him as he came out into the lounge. "The woman, uh, the one that came in yesterday, the drug OD from the homicide scene?" I raised my eyebrows. He shook his head, with a look that said it. "Yeah she uh, didn't make it. Unfortunate, but I don't think she had any acquaintances come over since last night. You were questioning her I assumed. You didn't know her did you?"

I felt like someone had just punched me in the gut. A hundred fast fading images flooded my brain, memories of my son growing up, memories I had never made with him, the husband I had forgotten to love somewhere along the journey, the one I'd made alone. I felt bile rise in my throat as I looked away from the doctor's face, the way I had looked away from every other question that I couldn't answer for a very long time.

"No. I didn't know her."

I turned and walked away, crushing the coffee cup in my fist like it was made of wafer. I didn't know what I felt; I just didn't want to feel anything.

I remembered the things she told me. I rubbed my hand where she'd held it. I wondered just who the hell she had been, to walk back into my life only to leave so soon. I hurled the crushed coffee cup at a trashcan, and kicked a stone on the pavement outside and sent it flying.

"There you are!" I turned to see my son, Trevor walking up to me, headphones around his neck, gum in his mouth and his phone in his hand, his fingers furiously and dexterously jabbing at it. "You FORGOT!" He yelled. "You're going to stand me up again aren't you," he said, more of a statement than a question.

I must have looked lost, because he looked angrier. I'd failed to notice how much Trevor had grown up and I saw now, awe-stricken that he really had. "You were supposed to come to the Back-to-School barbeque. My teachers are going to be there. The entire school is going to be there. Dad's busy so you said-"

"Of course," I heard myself say. "I was just, well, wrapping up things here. I'm coming."

"Huh, like, seriously?" He opened his mouth, and blew a gum bubble. I didn't know people could really do that. We were walking back to my cop-car and he was telling me how his lab-partner had made a volcano in chemistry and almost had it blow up in his face, and I was laughing, feeling my jaw-line, my facial muscles flex as if awakened after a long slumber.

"So uh," he glanced sideways at me as I backed the car out of parking. "So you're really coming this time?"

The walkie-talkie crackled to life, as if on cue, and sure enough I was gritting my teeth as Isaac's voice interrupted our profound moment. I sighed and placed a hand on the stupid thing, as if that was going to help. I watched Trevor's face fall from the corner of my eye. I turned and looked back at the hospital building, and I remembered Hailey's face.

I remembered her bright, earnest eyes, and everything she'd told me. She'd been there to watch the dawn of my motherhood unfold, because she'd made it happen. Then she'd disappeared, and after eleven years, I'd seen her again.

She'd told me what I'd needed to hear the most, that for all those times I'd failed my son, my husband and myself, I could be forgiven. Hailey had lived and died as a virtual stranger to me, but I'd remember her forever.

The sun had begun to set in the distance and the sky was darkening slowly. Birds were flying home. It was time for me to come home, too, I realized. To be more than Sheriff Lockheed of the town that looked up to me, to be what I'd always wanted to be, to be all of me.

To be my son's mother.

"Yeah Trev, I'll be there," I turned, smiling, "all the time from now."

THE END

5. THE MAN WHO BELIEVED

Nobody can really remember the whole of their lives. What we can remember are the moments that mattered, and the people who were in them. My mind was never really helpful when it came to recollecting formulae or memorizing dates and phone numbers, but when I met a person, I listened to them with all of my heart, and long after they left, I remembered the things they said, the way their eyes would shine, the gestures they made inadvertently, the way they smiled. I remembered.

For me life is like a collection of those conversations, and each person tells you something invaluable, something that you can never forget. In fact I don't think good or bad things happen to us. I think *people* happen to us.

I met Aaron Prince Kestler in college, but we didn't talk on a regular basis. In our last year of college when my self esteem had hit rock bottom with depression and I could only look back and see all the things I could have done, Aaron Kestler reemerged from wherever he had been for years, and he told me things that I'd never forget. He told me things that I so badly needed to hear then.

Aaron was and is the single most hopeful person I have ever met. He spoke with so much passion and intensity, about how much he longed to travel, meet people, and change their lives. I've heard a lot of people say a lot of things along those lines, but he wasn't like that. You could hear it in his voice; you could see it in his eyes. This man saw beauty everywhere, and he was bursting with happiness and hope. He loved trekking. When I saw Aaron in my mind I could only see him in an old t shirt and shorts with a bag on his shoulder and a bottle of water in his hand. I called him a gypsy.

He was the oldest person in class. He had dropped a couple of years to prepare for competitive exams. But in the end he was admitted in the same university as me and I will remain forever grateful for the day he'd walked into it because Aaron showed me you could have so much hope in you that sometimes you felt like you were floating. I have never really felt that. But I know I can, and I know this because of him.

He actually believed that every person had something to do in the world, and everything happened for a reason. At this point I'd ask something, like why so many innocent babies died for no fault of their own, and Aaron wouldn't miss a beat before telling me that I had no idea what could have happened to them if they were alive. None of us had a clue where the other person's life was headed to, he'd say. He believed in the butterfly effect. He said that no matter how bad things seem, there will always be a better time. And he believed this so fervently, that he would instantly make you want to believe it too.

Aaron Kestler's happiness was infectious. With him, everything was awesometastic. He told me that he'd sat all by himself in a room and broke into tears thinking of how blessed he was, feeling grateful for all the good things in life. Aaron sincerely wanted to tell people that they were amazing, to let them know how much they meant to the universe. He'd speak with so much joy exploding in his words, and he'd end them with a whisper that the world was just so beautiful.

And indeed it was. Aaron wished he could show people how to look at the world through his eyes. And I understood. I slowed down enough to see what was happening around me. Here was a man who was standing before destiny with so much of spirit, dying for adventure and actually capable of changing people's lives, and even he was afraid to be more than what he was then.

We had spirit in common; we had the thirst for adventure in common. But more than anything, we had fear in common. Aaron Kestler was frightened too, but he told me that the only real thing between us and our dreams were ourselves. He was convinced that nothing else could really keep us from becoming what we were meant to become. He held that our lives weren't programmed or planned to just follow a storyline but that we were writing it with each of our choices. That everything we thought, said and did would make the next part of our lives.

We'd both wanted to join the UN. We'd talk about it over coffee in college, about how we could really be a small part of huge changes even if we were just moving paperwork in the UN. We were afraid to imagine how it would be if we actually did it, but the idea thrilled us equally, I could tell. 'We'd be peacekeepers,' I'd tell him, and he would agree, relishing the thought.

What we didn't have in common was the love for food. Aaron ate food and I experienced food. It was the one thing he didn't see like I did, but he experienced life like I never could. We'd talk so much about all of it. I'd tell him I could show him how to appreciate food, and tell him to call me from all the places he traveled to, so that that I could tell him what to eat. Music was another thing Aaron loved with insane passion. I could never quite appreciate it the way he did.

Everything I said, Aaron understood. He really did, you know? He saw how afraid I was to open up and give myself a chance to open one of those doors for myself and see what lay ahead. I was just so very scared, and I was stuck. I was depressed, exhausted and haunted by my mistakes. I had no will left and my soul was trapped under a truckload of horseshit.

I needed advice, and Aaron Kestler wasn't even advising, he wasn't preaching, he wasn't teaching. He simply believed in happiness, and when you saw that kind of faith and conviction in someone's eyes, well. It is something to do with being a human being, I think. There's a part of us deep down that knows what is right. No matter what choice we make, I think at heart we always recognize what is right. And I knew that Aaron was right. We agreed that the greatest tragedy of humankind being sad and sorry was that if we looked closely enough, there really wasn't a reason good enough for it.

Aaron Kestler could make you love the world, despite all the horrible things that happen in it. He made you want to be adventurous knowing all the danger that could befall you. I can never forget how Aaron loved quoting the speech from Coach Carter, where the kid says that 'our deepest fear is not that we are inadequate. Our deepest fear is that we are powerful beyond measure.' He sincerely believed that we could bring about unimaginably astounding change in the world if we began with ourselves. And he longed to convince people of this.

We'd talk about how we could pack a bag and walk away one day, be a gypsy, see the world, and wherever we went, we'd tell people they were amazing. We'd make them realize how truly blessed they were and how much they meant to the world. Aaron convinced me I mattered. Now it is my turn, and wherever I go, whomever I meet, I've vowed to spend every moment I have with them to make them smile and never let go of hope; to show them that they matter.

In the movie The Great Gatsby, the narrator describes Gatsby as the most hopeful man he had ever met. During one of our most memorable conversations I blurted out, "Aaron, you're Gatsby. You're the Great Gatsby." And he smiled, the corners of his eyes crinkling up and I could see them shining with nothing but happiness that he'd managed to change something inside of me. Aaron and I connected, and he had more in common that most people did with me. I had spent my years in college being unhappy and feeling like I belonged nowhere, but with Aaron I knew I was being heard. He was a living testimony to the indomitable human spirit, and he was truly generous with hope. He just couldn't wait to give it to every person he met.

After graduation I left before anyone else, and I inevitably lost touch with most people and Aaron Kestler was one of them. I had no idea where he went or what happened to him, and I had no time to think about anybody for that matter. I was too busy building a life. And there's a part of me that regrets it, but the bigger part, the bully, adamantly refuses to believe I did anything wrong by leaving people behind without so much as a good bye.

* *

"Ma'am? You have a visitor." I pick up some of my files and slam them on the desk, irritated and angry at myself for wasting time I didn't have even though I knew I barely spent an hour of a day doing anything but work. "If it isn't on the schedule it isn't happening, Claire," I say shortly, deftly tapping at my keyboard without a moment's pause. I can vaguely hear Claire's pleas being ignored and security being called for. I don't even glance through the glass wall because I know it will be handled by people before I even begin to care. *"This is an office of the United Nations, Sir, we will be forced to remove you from the premises if you walk through that door..."*

"So. The UN and all, huh?" I look up, forgetting to breathe for a brief moment, when I took in the old t-shirt, the shorts, the bag and the bottle, the one day's stubble on his face. He is exactly as I remember, every detail the way I knew it would be, and his eyes shine bright the way they always had with innocent joy and boundless hope. I wave away a horrified Claire and am vaguely aware of two guards rushing toward us from the floors below.

"I told you that you were gonna be awesometastic one day," he said matter-of-factly and flopped down on the leather sofa to the other side of my spacious office, looking up at me like the last time we'd met was over lunch yesterday and not almost a decade ago.

Out of the corner of my eyes, I see Claire exchanging looks of bewilderment with one the guards. "Yeah," my face breaks into a grin as I nod. "Yeah man, you did."

THE END

6. LEAP OF FAITH

Our lives are made up of a million fleeting moments. Sometimes we act on the spur of a moment and things work like magic, sometimes we regret them. We wish they'd never happened. But most often, it is when we seize the magic of these moments, that looking back, we realize a memory was born, right then, right there. No matter how afraid we are, ten years from then that moment will probably give us all the faith we'd ever need.

And I know this, because I knew Joe Black. Tall, heavy-set and broad-shouldered, he was then thirty three years old and often thought his name was a joke. Raised in an African-American colony in Arizona, he had no idea who his father was, but he'd liked to imagine that he just didn't have one. That he was somehow a magic child. That somehow he hadn't been born of rape like many others there. He hoped fervently that every day when his mother looked at him, she didn't see him as a horrifying reminder of a painful past. That somehow he hadn't been a child that could and would have been killed if not for destiny.

The only things he remembered from his childhood were the smell of the fresh bread that his mother baked, and the vague picture of her in her checked apron splotched with sauce. Joe had always found her beautiful in her apron. But then he wanted to remember no more, because his memory had been scarred by things that a child should never have survived.

When Joe was six years old, he'd been playing with the other little black children in the neighbourhood when he heard a loud bang followed by the sound of shattering glass. He ran inside, to watch his mother struggle against a man he did not recognize, and he'd watched her get shot. He'd watched her fall, and he'd stood cowering in fear until the man had left. When he edged closer to his mother's lifeless form then, the apron was stained with more than sauce and the smell of blood had taken over that of warm bread. Little Joe had fled home, and that was the last day of his entire life that he'd been a child.

After years on the streets, living out of boxes and garbage cans, Joe knew that the only person that hadn't made him feel ugly would always be his dead mother, and every time the world jeered at him in one way or another, Joe told himself the same. He was growing bigger and stronger but definitely not less ugly. He yearned to love and be loved, and to matter. But he knew that no one who could see would ever want to know him. No one who had eyes that saw him would ever love him. He didn't look particularly lovable and he just knew it.

So when Joe Black trudged up the stairs to his empty flat one New Year's eve, he felt nothing in particular except immense fatigue. He flicked on the lights and grumpily kicked a take-out box out of his way. Joe looked around, taking in his little home, a familiar mess, mirroring his life. He'd been busy and his bones ached for the bed. He would watch a movie, a comedy, he decided. "An' bloody well get a good laugh," he told no one in particular, and the emptiness glared back at him. He ordered Mexican, and went into the shower. When he had put food down his throat and downed a can of coke, he stood at the window and looked out at the street.

Tomorrow would be another year, the beginning of some things and the end of some, for everyone else in the world. Joe sighed, knowing that it wouldn't be a thing different for him. He'd come back to this little flat, after having driven across town carrying dead people and parcel boxes with the same casual air. Joe knew that for people who cared it probably meant a world of a difference but he had been alone too long to care.

Somewhere along the movie, Joe fell fast asleep. He was rudely awakened by the shrill ringing of his phone and he took a couple of seconds to open his eyes even though he knew that he couldn't stop the stupid thing from ringing. "Yeah?" he answered with obvious annoyance. "It's Lou, mate."

Oh, Lord, no, thought Joe. Here it comes.

"Between 3rd and 4th, Walter de la Mare Street," Lou told him the address without preamble. Joe had taken a lot of odd jobs to survive until Lou found him this job as a truck driver at this parcel company, but then as a return of the favour Lou would occasionally call him to pick up a corpse or even a casualty. It worked both ways because Lou could use the extra help, Joe was the only one without a family and the money was good.

Out of the corner of his eye, Joe noticed a bug crawl out of one of his take-out boxes which were forming a sizeable pile by the moth-eaten couch. He squashed it under his foot angrily. "Yeh've a clue what time it is, buddy? It's New Year's goddamn it!" He could hear Lou smile at the other end. "I'm sorry, mate. It's an emergency, there's been a fire down at the factory, and we had the boys down there, man. Now they'll all probably be drunk."

"That's too bad man but ah ain't no doctor! Ah don't do emergencies in the middle of the night," Joe exploded. "Hey hey calm down. Just get your ass down here and take the keys," Lou told him and he heard the clang of keys being slammed on the table. "No one down there, mate," Lou remarked when Joe remained silent. "Some poor dead guy, freezing on his own, on New Year's Eve…"

"Fine! Fine ah'll go!" Joe yelled exasperatedly.

"Happy new year, mate!" Lou was grinning now.

"Oh cork it, Lou," Joe hung up, shaking his head.

He had a steaming mug of coffee waiting for him when Joe walked into the town's only hospital, and it helped tremendously. What saddened him was that he knew what Lou was thinking. *You're the only one without family, mate... you're the only one who would work holidays...*

But Joe said nothing. He drained his coffee while talking to Lou and pocketed the keys to the tiny town hospital's only battered ambulance, and then he got into it and drove off. It was freezing outside and there wasn't any music so Joe resorted to talking to himself to keep him entertained. It had begun to snow, and Joe loved snow. He was watching little flakes dance around and land all around as he drove by to pick up the corpse of a man he'd never known, when he thought he'd heard a muffled scream.

He continued driving because, you know, whatever, tomorrow was New Year's, people were probably celebrating very loudly or something and uh, screaming out of pleasure perhaps? But then he slowed down, imagining horrible things. What if somebody was actually getting hurt and he was going to read it in the paper the next day knowing that he had driven Lou's crappy ambulance by the same place and hadn't stopped because he was just being a deluded moron?

Joe reversed the van and decided to check the coast. That's when he saw them, a bunch of drunken men hardly visible in the mist. Then he heard it again, the scream. Oh Lord, I can't fight them bastards, he thought. Joe was terrified. He hated fights. He could still go, and no one would know...

But the idea that there was somebody in the middle of that just frightened him beyond the fear of confronting them, so he squared his shoulders and went down on the gas for all that he was worth, rolling onto the snow and preparing to ram the van into some empty tar cans right in front of the men.

He saw their startled eyes in front of the headlights and he watched their faces tense as he gave them one look, and the next he knew, he had sent them scampering into darkness. He jammed the brakes, got out and looked around, his heart pounding in his ears like it had when he'd heard the gunshots back in Arizona. "Holy…" a gasp left his lips when he saw who the muggers had left behind.

She was the most beautiful thing Joe had ever seen up close, and he took his eyes off her face only to make sure the wolves weren't lurking around. Thick black hair spilled onto the snow all around her, and her lips were blue from cold. She was wounded to her head and her bag lay open beside her. Her eyes were half open and entreating, but somewhere in them he knew that he frightened her too. Joe picked her up and swung her onto his back effortlessly, bending to pick up her bag before getting back to his van.

So that's how the unidentified corpse between 3rd and 4th, Walter de la Mare Street never got picked up that night, and that's how Joe Black's year began.

* *

Joe took her to the town hospital and ignored an exasperated Lou when he gave him back the keys. "Ah know the difference between a dead person and one that's still fighting," Joe told him. "You were supposed to do what you're getting paid for," Lou fired back, lowering his voice as a nurse turned to stare, "instead of playing the iron man! Now who's going to answer the cops?"

Joe wasn't sure he cared, really. He just couldn't forget those few minutes of the previous night when he'd been part of something that this girl would wake up to call a miracle. He couldn't believe that in a lifetime of being pushed around and living out of carton boxes, of being more unwanted than the garbage he'd eaten out of, he'd made that miracle happen. He'd actually saved someone's life!

Joe shook his head, walking toward the coffee machine. "Ah'll tell 'em what ah know, Lou."

The doctor told him that the only wound she had was on her head, where she'd collided with something hard and she was otherwise unhurt. She was identified as Iara Garcia, the Brazilian girl who had been reported missing two days ago. She'd run away from her home after a fight, according to her family, and then she'd apparently been staying at a friends', before she left there too and become absconding.

Joe wanted to look at her, but the nurses wouldn't let him because he wasn't family. More because I look like a bear, he thought as he sat back. The little nurses were visibly threatened by his presence and he was only too familiar with that. The cops were pretty rough with him too, and that, again, he'd grown up with.

When Iara woke up, she asked for him and Joe was afraid to go in because I mean, when was the last time somebody wasn't repelled by him? Whatever was going to happen in there, he had to go in and face it. So he did.

She was propped up against pillows and her hair framed a beautiful face with almond eyes and honey colored skin. When he walked in, she looked up and beamed the brightest smile he'd seen in thirty three years. "Is your name Joseph Black?" she asked, the smile unwavering.

Joe said something really intelligent like "Uhm, hmm," but frankly I don't think he remembered his name at that point. "Please," she beckoned, "come in." Joe let himself in but remained quiet.

"Did you save my life?"

"Yer alive," Joe found courage to say.

"That's true," she nodded, bemusedly surveying this big man. "Yer eyes smile," he managed, and then he watched her blush. Joe had never made anybody blush in his entire life. Cringe in disgust, check, but not blush.

"I ran away from home. I'm glad you found me. Or else I'd probably be dead now," she said matter-of-factly, and Joe shuddered. "Yeh shouldn't have done that," he said disapprovingly. "Yeh should neva walk away from yer family."

"I know, I'm sorry. I shouldn't have."

"Ah don't have no family," remarked Joe.

"You're such a nice person, why would you be alone? What about a girlfriend?" Iara asked curiously.

"Ya really hit yer head, dintcha," Joe declared. Her laughter sounded like heaven.

* *

Gradually Iara healed, and Joe visited every day. The nurses began to be at ease with him and when Iara told them she wasn't pressing charges against anybody, one of the cops even gave him a pat on his back. That was more positivity than Joe had got from fair-skinned policemen all his life.

Iara was like a ball of happiness, and she just had this effect on people around her. She honestly didn't seem to notice that Joe looked like a hideous beast next to her stunning self and she'd talk endlessly until the nurse reprimanded her for not resting. One day Joe tramped in with snow on his boots and all over his head and jacket, and the nurses frowned at the trail he left behind him. Iara just beckoned him closer and brushed the flakes off his head, and he beamed.

"What," she asked, laughing.

"S' funny," he shook his head, but she wasn't letting go. "Come on, tell me!" she'd never let go easily. "S' funny, but ah feel safe when yeh do stuff like that," he admitted reluctantly. Iara threw back her head and laughed, shaking her head. "That's crazy, I mean, you're this big strong guy and I brush snow off your head and you feel safe?" Joe shrugged his massive shoulders. "Ah told yeh s' funny, s' hard to understand, but s' true."

"Believe you me, that is hard to imagine," Iara never stopped laughing. The sound of her laughter was like a song, it was stuck in his head and it made him hum at work and Lou thought he was crazy and the entire world treated him like it had always done, and yet, nothing mattered. Nothing did because the world, despite all its hostility, had given him a friend.

"Yeh light up when yeh see me," he told Iara one day. "What's weird about that?" she blinked, completely oblivious to all the things about his looks that sent other people running. "Are yeh blind?" he asked, and she erupted into laughs again. "I'm not blind, goodness, no," she said breathlessly between laughs, and she leaned back to look at him. "Tell me one word that you'd describe yourself with," she said.

"Ugly," Joe said without blinking. "Ugly as shit, ah say." More peals of laughter.

"Who told you that? Look at you, now, you have the looks of a, let's see, a secret agent, you know? Like a tough cop guy. You could totally go to Hollywood, yeah," she concluded, nodding. Joe made a face, but she'd never let go. She'd win every argument and there'd be no instant when a shadow crossed her face.

"People do notice each other because of the way they look, that's true," she nodded, "but no matter how hot you think someone's ass is, or whatever, all of that will fade over time. Character will remain for you to fall in love with, over and over again."

"Ah say that's a loada sad shit," Joe disagreed, but Iara wasn't letting go. "It's true, you'll know. Character is what you'd do for people who can't do anything for you. Like when you picked me up that night when I couldn't possibly do a thing in return for you. That's what's in you, and that will be heard no matter what's on the outside; which isn't bad by the way, throw in a pair of sunglasses and a coat, there you go, Mr. G. I. Joe," she teased. "S' stupid, that is," he grinned.

"So what's the one word you'd use to describe me?" she asked curiously. "Happiness," it took him no effort to say. Iara's laughter was priceless.

She was the best thing that had ever happened to him. He thought about her all the time and sometimes he wondered if this strange little friendship was something more than what it looked like.

But Joe didn't know what love looked like, so he couldn't tell. When it came to love, Joe was like a child who'd never been to the sea, but knew that it was big and beautiful and sometimes scary and dangerous, all from tales.

The night before she was leaving, Joe Black could have passed easily for the saddest man on earth. Iara, on the other hand was as happy as she'd been the first day after being mugged and almost murdered. "Hey, big man. Why the long face?" Iara teased, and watching her, Joe had a lump in his throat.

"Come here," she beckoned, and he sat beside her so that she could lie on his shoulder. She took his hand and hers looked tiny next to it. He tried to pull back, but she said 'shh...' and continued to hold his hand.

Joe knew instantly, that he'd remember that moment for the rest of his life.

"Will ah see yeh again?" he asked her the next day when she stood on her toes to give him a hug and he had to be careful not to crack her ribs as he almost lifted her off the ground. "Of course, because hey, I like a man who can literally sweep me off my feet," she winked, and her eyes seemed to sparkle. "I'm going to miss you, Joe," she told him kindly. "You saved my life."

"An' ya saved mine," Joe replied, his booming voice breaking in gratitude. Big drops of tears made their way down his face as he stood waving goodbye to Iara. "Hey, hey," she squeezed his massive hand one last time before the car backed out, and Joe stood watching.

He watched until it was out of sight, and he walked back to his little flat, knowing that Iara Garcia was his own personal miracle, the way he had been hers that New Year's.

That he had all the faith he would ever need, because of one blind leap he'd made.

THE END

7. TWENTY FOUR HOURS

Some days aren't like the rest. They come seemingly ordinary, but when they're gone, life is no longer the same. Something inside of you changes, perhaps forever. From then on, you remember your life as before that day, and after.

When Danielle walked into her office building that morning, everything was the same as it had always been. She glanced callously at faces, everyone in a hurry like she had always seen them, just like herself. It was just another ordinary, insufferable day. "Danielle Swinton," she barked into the phone as she walked inside the lobby of Sparks and Grey Publishing House. "I cannot believe this," she resumed angrily.

"Why is my secretary absconding, why is there no replacement yet, and why," she paused, her eyes reducing to dangerous slits as she glared at the construction workers who were merrily at their jobs early in the morning, "am I carrying my own coffee," she spat.

"Mornin' Danielle!" Frankie, the electrician called out hopefully to her like he did every day. Danielle ignored him like she did every day, and barked at the human resources manager clinging onto the phone with his ear a foot away, understandably threatened by this vicious woman.

She stepped into the elevator and clicked the pointy ends of her Prada on the floor impatiently. "I'm completely apologetic, Danielle I'm so sorry this is happening to you," Craig Portman, the human resources manager, like all rational human beings, did not appreciate being woken up before his time on any given day with a thirty year old woman wailing over the phone as if her tooth was being extracted without an anesthetic.

Portman had known Danielle for a quite a while now, and he knew Sparks and Grey kept her because she was so damn good at what she did, and also, because there were only about another dozen people who wanted her for her skill. People in the business, people who smiled and clinked glasses at work parties.

They'd whisk Danielle away in the blink of an eye, and that's why it was completely worth it to put up with every single one of her tantrums, because they weren't just tantrums, they were predicaments that needed resolving, and that is what people like Portman did. Which was precisely the reason he was apologizing to this woman right then, despite undeniable evidence of her insanity. "We didn't know in time to do anything, I mean I woke up this morning and there was no mail, no note on my desk, no message telling me a replacement was required-"

"Do I sound like someone who cares?" Danielle cut him off. "Where's my replacement, well, nowhere because of your incompetency, I got that, now this girl, whatshername, where is she?" "Her name's Melissa and her father passed away." Danielle was now in the elevator.

"Well I am sorry but I am terminating the girl with the dead dad because people do NOT just disappear from work because of any reason at all! And I would send you home and shut down your entire department as well if they would let me, because I am not here to put up with this kind of complete and utter lack of sensitivity," she spat. Portman shook his head in disbelief. Look who's talking about sensitivity.

"Danielle, I'm sorry but for chrissake the man had been jogging when he'd a heart attack, how was anyone to know-"

"Craig, Craig," Danielle interrupted calmly. The elevator doors pinged open and people rolled their eyes as Danielle Swinton walked into her office on Level 9. "This is your cue to shut the hell up and get your ass back to work. And while you're at it, ask your wife to fish your brains out from under the bills in the salad bowl where you put it there last night and USE it. In other words, turn around and mail me a list of people to be interviewed for the post of the girl with the dead dad and send in a temporary replacement for until then that I will not have to fire in the next two hours hopefully. And-"

"I'm sorry Danielle."

Click. Portman knew the conversation was over.

Danielle threw her coat on the chair and banged her handbag on her desk, placing her coffee on the table. She took a sip and nearly spat it out because it had gone slightly cooler than her regular, which was scalding.

She dialed the lobby on the office phone and waited. "Alan? Danielle Swinton. Of course you know. Yes you can, and you better. See that guy there, the one in the orange elevator guy's costume? Yes that's your Frankie. You go there and tell him I know he has a crush on me and he's had it since forever but the next time I pass by the lobby, tell him to disappear or I will cut his balls off and feed them to the pigeons. That will be all, thank you."

Danielle turned in her chair on hearing someone clear their throat. A young, fine looking man stood panting, holding her glass door open with one foot and balancing a tray of Starbucks, a jacket, a briefcase and a folder. He looked positively petrified, obviously having heard the last line. Her lips parted in the tiniest smile, the best Danielle ever gave. "Come on in," she beckoned.

"Well hello there, I'm Rick, how are you doing?" he said warmly, holding out his hand expectantly. Danielle looked at it blankly. He looked at it too, and for a painfully embarrassing couple of seconds they both just looked at his hand until he withdrew it. "Go again," Danielle said. "What?" "I said, go again. Introduce yourself again."

Rick looked thrown. "Good morning, my name is Rick and I'm here to, uh be interviewed for the post of your secretary and I still want to know how you are, you know, uh." Rick shrugged. Danielle exhaled sharply. "For starters, this is not a radio show, and stop saying 'uh' every five seconds, and also, how I am is none of your business. Do you have a last name?"

Rick nodded, shocked. "Of course. Wolf. Rick Wolf." He tried to hand her his bio but she dismissed it with a wave. "Give me answers, okay, Mr. Wolf? Speak to me like your life depends on it." Rick gaped. From where he came, people didn't talk this way.

"Now, what is it that you did before you came here?"

"I brushed my teeth and put on my pants," Rick said without missing a beat.

Danielle gritted her teeth and decided to let it go. "I mean, for a living," she said slowly. Rick shifted uncomfortably. "Just, you know, this and that, the odd job."

"One more time," Danielle was clenching her fists under the desk, "what was your occupation before you chose to attempt to fill this vacancy?" she repeated slowly, as if he were a dyslexic child.

"I was a teaching assistant."

Danielle wanted to pin Craig Portman to her wall and throw darts at him.

"Well, I see how easy this is going to be," she muttered to no one in particular as she glared at the phone. There was no one else to be interviewed and a replacement wasn't available for Danielle Swinton's assistant's position.

People were truly terrified of filling it even if bills needed to be paid. Also, Melissa had already emailed human resources along with a letter from the staff counseling cell which Danielle barely looked at, but catching words like 'emotionally traumatizing superiors' and 'would rather eat dung than spend another day with the [beep]ing [beep]' and you get the gist.

So her only option was this person sitting before her.

"Look here now, Mr. Wolf. I will be interviewing people for this vacancy as soon as they start coming in after you, so you do realize you are just a temporary substitute for the person who will inevitably come. Do you?" Danielle glared. Rick nodded. "Well, alright then. That's your desk right there, and your job is to keep me happy. Are we clear on that?"

Rick went, "I'm sorry, what would that involve?" Danielle shot him a look before answering.

"Man the desk. Answer the phone. Schedule and re-schedule meetings the way I want. Get my breakfast. Do the first three again and then get my lunch. Oh and coffee," she nodded, turning away and scrolling through her e-mails and frowning already, "Starbucks, as hot as it comes. Anything less than that and I will watch you go back and get me a fresh cup." She wasn't even looking at him.

"You could just order it, you know. They have this office order thing," Rick offered helpfully, leaning forward, but pulling back instantly as she turned to fix him with a steely stare. "I will assume I did not just hear that," she said with an air of dismissal, nodding toward her coffee cup. Rick picked it up and left the room quietly. She had not touched it.

So thus began another day in Sparks and Grey. Danielle Swinton was a bitch and everyone knew that, accepted it and moved on. Every day she walked into the very same building, shot unfriendly glares to the very same employees, and rode the very same elevator up and down.

Every day, people around her wished it would be different. Every day their prayers went heaven-ward unanswered. Danielle Swinton remained a bitch, and well, people are what they are.

At 1 o' clock that day Danielle had a meeting with Leo Prentice, the Senior Editorial Advisor. Danielle contemplated a raise in her salary as she strode into the elevator. She clicked her heels against the floor of the elevator car as usual and checked her watch approximately every two minutes.

As it left Level 35, the elevator groaned, and refused to move any further up. Danielle clicked her tongue. Leo was not someone she wanted to keep waiting. Three minutes later, she banged on the wall of the car, and it shook slightly. "Hello," she called dubiously. "Anybody there?"

Another minute passed and she lifted her finger to jab the emergency button. It wasn't working. "Darn," she cursed and took her phone out, only to discover that she had no signal. "You're shitting me," she shook her head and punched the emergency button hard, recoiling and flexing her fingers.

She turned toward the camera and waved. "Somebody get this thing moving!" Nothing happened. She turned to the doors and she could see through the crack that she was halfway up to Level 35. "Hey!" she yelled into the intercom, pressing buttons in vain. She glanced at her watch. I'm late, she thought. Ten minutes and there wasn't a peep from security.

"Listen UP," she yelled into the camera, "Get your asses down here and make this damn thing WORK!" Still nothing.

Fifteen minutes. Danielle stepped out of her heels and threw them across from her angrily, leaning against the side of the elevator. Half an hour later, there was still no word from the security. Danielle sat down with a sigh. She was beginning to worry.

What a damned day, first the girl with the dead dad and then the teaching assistant and now this? Damn them all! "I'll get you fired! FIRED!" she yelled at no one in particular. It exhausted her to sit still and not be able to do anything. It was soon three quarters of an hour, and then an hour.

Just when she was wondering if it could get any worse, the lights went out. "Yeah, screw YOU too!" she yelled, and then she forced herself to calm down. The power had been switched off because they were working on it, perhaps? That was good, because that meant help was on its way.

Hours had passed since Danielle had got trapped in the elevator, and soon she wanted to throw up. When she had calmed down, the anger disappeared and fear took its place. Sitting in darkness, on the floor of the elevator, Danielle began to sing. She always thought she sang terribly, but today it didn't matter.

Today nothing mattered, because today was different. The sound of her voice bounced off the walls in an eerie silence. Danielle was comforting herself with the world's worst rendition of Madonna's 'Quicker than a Ray of Light,' when she thought she saw a spark through the crack between the doors.

She thought she had imagined it but there it was, again. Fire, she thought instantly. There's been a short circuit and it's going to catch fire. "Oh my God!" she shouted, trying to get up and stumbling on the pile that was her coat and bag, falling. She swore aloud as a sharp pain shot up her ankle.

"Please," she cried out, clutching her ankle. "Please do something," she turned blindly to what she knew would be the surveillance camera. She heard a hissing noise and saw the spark through the crack again. "*Please*," she begged, unable to control tears. "Help me, please, somebody," she was sobbing now.

It felt like forever since she'd been trapped and a claustrophobia she knew she didn't have struck her. Danielle felt ensnared and she imagined the walls closing in on her. She heard the hissing noise again, and fear seeped in from corners of her mind. Her throat was parched and her head had begun to ache from fear and anxiety.

Danielle fumbled about for her phone and jabbed at it, hoping that somehow a signal had been restored, but it hadn't, to her dismay. Desperately she clicked on her voice mail because she wanted to hear voices, someone in the world other than her at that point. Fifteen messages.

The first two messages were from Leo's secretary reminding her about the meeting and the third from Leo wondering if she could please make it fast, the next two from Rick confirming her meeting at one and then asking her, was everything alright, did she need to reschedule? All in a matter of minutes from each call. The next was Rick again, slightly worried. The next was Leo's secretary to finally tell her that the meeting had been postponed indefinitely and that Leo was not happy.

The list went on and there were voices, cold unfeeling voices, her unhappy subordinates asking her for signatures, approval of cover, draft of editorial, permission to run through the cover story for fashion, approval of final edits… Then there was a message from home, and as she listened to her mother's voice, Danielle burst into fresh sobs.

She hadn't gone home in months and didn't call. She'd missed the last wedding and had her assistant send an apologetic email. Her mother's lovely familiar voice rang through the stillness of the elevator car, and she was telling him how the dog had puppies, and how beautiful they were. 'I'm making pie. Honey and apple,' she said finally, sounding unsure. 'Come home, honey. We miss you so much...' Click. Her phone complained that it was running low on battery and then it died, and her stomach rumbled loudly.

"I miss you too, mum," she said, sobbing. I'll come; she thought to herself, I promise I will, if I make it out alive. There was a spark again. "Help, oh, God, please," she cried. "I'll pray, I will!" she mumbled aloud, and then, struck by the absurdity of it all, Danielle began laughing hysterically.

She dabbed at her cheeks and imagined her tear-streaked face, what a monstrosity she must look! Leo will sack me, she thought. I've missed the meeting, and it will not matter because I'll be dead, she thought as she laughed. "You can't fire a dead person, hear that?" she yelled, laughing again.

Then the laughter died down and made way for quiet tears again, because she could see how happy everyone would be if she wasn't there anymore. She could see it now, her empty desk, and people walking into work with happy smiles. She would be dead, and the world would be the same as it was every day.

It was then, as Danielle Swinton sat in the dark, on the floor of the elevator, holding her twisted ankle and sobbing like a child, that something changed, inside of her. She was no longer that powerful insensitive she-devil; she was helpless and distraught, she was crying and laughing as a thousand faces flickered before her. She remembered everyone who'd walked into her life, who'd tried to stay, and how she'd driven them away.

It was then, as those memories flooded her mind that Danielle Swinton thought of the smiles she'd never had time for, of the kind words she'd kept for another day, and all the gifts she'd never given. "I want pie," she mumbled quietly, no more aware of what she was saying, and then she burst into peals of laughter listening to herself.

Helpless was not a word she'd ever attributed to herself, and yet here she was. And it hurt to know that it didn't matter to anybody out there if tomorrow came and she wasn't there.

"I want pie," she repeated, and before she knew it, Danielle had lost consciousness. She fell asleep and did not wake for hours.

* *

Long after, she was vaguely aware of lights flickering back on. The tip of something like a crowbar appearing between the elevator doors, and in seconds someone was forcing it open as she blinked stupidly in the sudden flood of light. She heard voices and saw faces, each of them anxious to know if she was safe. "Good Lord, thank God!" "Back off, people, make room, now!" "Its fine, she's okay!"

Danielle saw a flash of orange, and holding the crowbar with a triumphant smile was Frankie the electrician, the one she'd threatened and ignored for as long as she could remember.

The elevator was indeed stuck half-way to the next level and looking down at her and preparing to lift her out with his open arms was Rick Wolf, the under-qualified teaching assistant she had barely just met. Hovering around anxiously were more familiar faces, whom she had seen every day and forgotten in a wink. Names she had never bothered to learn. Friends she had never cared enough to make.

"Alright, alright, thank *God*!" Rick had her in his big strong arms for a minute before a medic strapped her to a stretcher, but he gave her a reassuring nod. A strangely familiar girl in braces and glasses was gesturing wildly with her hands and apologizing profusely and Danielle had no clue what she was saying. "Who-?" she managed to croak, vaguely registering green bands on her braces.

"Uh, Melissa, your assistant?" the girl offered, taken aback, and that was the last Danielle saw before she collapsed in exhaustion. Hours later, when she had glucose in her bloodstream and had slept for some time, she woke up to find Rick sitting beside her, having waited there all along. "How long was I in there?"

"A day, Danielle, an entire day! And Lord, it was crazy out there; they've no idea why it happened. There was nothing wrong with the elevators!"

"What about the fire?" She whispered, but Rick looked at her strangely. "There *was* no fire, Danielle. We just didn't know where you were because the security cameras got stuck at the last image and there was a mix up. Then we lost connection to them. There was no power in the entire building and they just couldn't do anything. It's unbelievable. No one knows what happened."

If there had been no fire, then what had she seen? What were those sparks and that hissing noise? A hallucination?

"But hey, listen, it doesn't matter, you're safe now. Go back to sleep," he said kindly.

For once in a lifetime of having been annoyingly stubborn, Danielle did exactly as she was told, only because she was still too exhausted to think.

The following week she turned up like a lost kitten on her parents' doorstep, and when she saw their faces crinkling into warm smiles, when she walked into a home full of familiar smells, she knew. She knew that every day in life mattered.

She knew that she would remember that one day forever, and how every sight in the world had suddenly seemed brighter, after twenty four hours in complete darkness.

THE END

8. I THINK...

Okay, so maybe the doctor's right. I *have* got to cut it out. I'm just going to relax and not think about anything for some time. Let me check the water in the bath, yeah, just the right kind of warm. God, what kind of bath stuff has he bought? Hmm, this one smells nice, fruity. I like fruity. Okay, in you go. Now, this was a tough week. I'm just going to step into this warm, bubbly, fruity-smelling bath and forget the whole world. Not a thought, not a worry.

How dare he say I'm bordering on insane, anyway? And hello, I do NOT think too much. Wow look at that big bubble go. It's so pretty. And he said if I didn't stop thinking all the time, I'd need anxiety pills. Bah! What does he know? He probably sucked at medical school. I should ask his medical school teachers. He probably couldn't even spell anxiety. No, that's too simple. Anybody can spell anxiety. Pneumonia! He probably couldn't spell pneumonia.

Oh God, Alistair's brother's breaking up, the one who had the girl friend who thought she got pneumonia when all she had was dust allergy from all the moving in. So obviously he's breaking up with that girl. Or was that before the one with the purple hair? Why does she have purple hair anyway? What is she, like, fifteen? And she's a lawyer, isn't she? Whoever knew they had purple haired lawyers? I mean, like, how does a judge take you seriously when your hair is purple? Is that why they're breaking up, because of the hair? Geez, you can dye the damn hair can't you. It's HAIR, not the end of the world.

Damn, why is all my hair falling off. Like, so much of it, you know? That's why I went to the doctor. But then he says its stress, blah. Did I turn off the stove? And anyway I don't work all the time. I'm only an engineer. I mean, don't doctors have more work pressure than engineers? No wonder doctors are so full of it, you know? Like that guy who Kia ended up dumping because he kept saying he was in surgery every time she called and then it turned out he was actually sleeping with the nurses. I mean not *all* of them, obviously. Just the two of them she found on top of him. In the surgery room actually, geez, I'm sorry but that's funny.

That reminds me, gosh, his mother's going into surgery next Friday. Or was it the Friday after that? I don't know. What do I get her? She's allergic to flowers. She never eats anything sweet. She hates presents which haven't been designed for her, built for her, discovered for her, named after her, or flown in for her. And she's going in for plastic surgery, just for the heck of it. And she's not even nice, you know? I mean the last time I met her, she said there are too many engineers in the world and they're probably all very stupid if there are so many more coming in. Seriously, what do you say to something like that? She's a nightmare.

He had this nightmare the other day and all he said is we were in Paris and then his boss turned up. He wouldn't say where. It disturbs me. Did he come to our hotel? Did he come to a party? Was he on the flight? Did he fall off the Eiffel Tower and die? I mean seriously, what? Do you not need to tell people details anymore? And what is it with bosses anyway? They're just so mean. And the part where they get paid all that money to be mean? That's ghastly.

My goodness, I just remembered, my paycheck is in the salad bowl. Why the hell is my paycheck in the salad bowl? I have got to get it out of there. Shucks I almost slipped there. Where's my towel? Why is this towel orange? Who buys an orange towel, like, seriously? I should never have let him buy the towels.

And look at this table cloth. It has a steak on it. I am a vegetarian! Do I want my table to have pictures of tiny little steaks hanging off it? That would be a no. And what is with everybody and my vegetarianism? Why is everybody telling me to 'get some flesh'? Even the doctor told me that. He said a person who thinks so much should definitely eat meat to have something substantial to burn before their head explodes. Like, seriously? I don't want to eat meat! Ugh! Everybody should be vegan like me. His mother had the audacity to say that it's boring and just not acceptable. I mean how is vegetarianism boring? And yeah, eating what used to walk around and make noises IS acceptable? How is THAT acceptable? HOW DOES THE WORLD NOT SEE THAT SHE'S A CRAZY WOMAN?

Okay, I'll have a drink. That should calm me down. A glass of red wine every day is good for health. And maybe I'll eat an apple. Ow, that hurt. I have got to find time for the dentist. Shit, I'm out of wine. Fine I'll have some OJ. Um, that's empty too. Then why is it still in the refrigerator? Who keeps an empty OJ carton in their refrigerator? And who calls it OJ? Ugh. I'll just have water. Why did I come here anyway? Oh yes, the salad bowl. That is a sad, *sad* paycheck. I have got to work harder. Maybe they'll give me a raise if I put in some more hours. After I see the dentist, obviously. I can't even figure out which tooth hurts, ouch. You know who else should see the dentist? His mother. Then the whole world will know she has fangs and is secretly a vampire.

And to top it all there's a book on the coffee table that says 'Home Decoration for Dummies'. I mean the man wanted green curtain with the daisies on them. That tells it. I'm married to a color-blind Resource Manager with the Godzilla for a mother and absolutely no idea about any of it. I have to call in and tell them the doctor gave me a day off before I forget. A day off work for thinking too much, do you believe this guy? There goes one more day's pay. What are they trying to do, diminish my salary to the size of a grape and then squash it?

Grape soda, yum. Do I have any grape soda? I'll go get some. That's what I should do, take a walk. Buy supplies. What else do I have to get? New towels? A new table cloth? New couch? A new HOUSE? If he buys one more piece of intolerably ugly furniture, I will lose it, seriously. And what's this? There are so many notes stuck on the refrigerator that I was worried he bought a yellow refrigerator. Knowing him, trust me, he could have. What do we have here; hmm...'Get milk'. Oh, here it is, 'get wine'. 'Mom- surgery, Friday'. I know it's on Friday, which damn Friday??? And who's Evelyn McKay and why is her phone number stuck to my refrigerator? Oh shit, that's the dentist.

And you know what else the doctor told me? He suggested I go see a shrink! Ugh. I *so* do not need to. All I need is to go to work. And if he won't let me do that, I'll just go out and get milk and wine and OJ and grape soda. And you know what else I'll buy? Vegetables. That should give his mother a coronary; the next time she comes over and opens the refrigerator and find out all we have are vegetables. I'll make her a vegetable soup, vegetarian lasagna, and for dessert she can have a grapefruit. Ha. HA.

Grapefruit... Grape soda? That was what I was going to buy, wasn't it? Right. I'll just get my coat. The paper's here. I hate reading the paper. The only section where someone's not dead is the Sports page, and that's only because you can't, you know, kill people when you lose against them. What's this? Gabriella is having a sale! Boots! Wait, I got boots. Coats! But his mother gave me this coat and she'll probably kill me if I don't wear it my whole life. I can *have* one more, can't I? Geez, can't a girl buy a coat? Where *is* my coat anyway? Ah, here it is. I'll read the rest of the paper when I come back.

Keys? Got them. Phone? Eleven messages! Oh look, he's texted to ask if I'm doing okay! That is so sweet. Husbands are nice people, you know. Even the ones that read 'Home Decoration for Dummies' and then get you orange colored towels. I'll text him back about the doctor and how he thinks I think too much. But then he thinks I think too much too. My husband, not the doctor. I mean the doctor obviously does, I'm saying my husband agrees with the doctor. Aaargh.

What is wrong with everybody? I'll just go back to work tomorrow. Do I think too much? Nah... I probably don't think *enough*.

THE END

PART II

Another Time,
Another Place

This part of the book contains stories written from the ages 11 to 14.
From innocence to understanding- it has been an incredible journey.

9. EVERMORE LOVE, EMMY

Everybody knew about Emmy Sparks and Jake Ashton. They were best friends as children. Their mums had tea parties together. Their dads played pool together. They went to school together. They grew up beside each other, racing each other everywhere yet never once without stopping to hold out a hand when one of them had fallen. Things were different back then in England. Sophistication, pride and pretence mattered too much then, at least it did to the grownups. Not to Emmy and Jake, though.

So everybody knew Emmy was meant for Jake and him for her. During their senior year, their mothers began to take an immense dislike to one another. It wasn't something unexpected; the two ladies had often had their differences. There were subtle changes in the scene that everyone failed to notice, or simply ignored. Jake didn't seem interested in pretty much anything that normal kids did, according to the adults. Emmy's mum tormented Mrs. Ashton with questions about her irresponsible boy, and the distance grew. They did nothing to help it.

Jake had taken an insane interest in music, writing and playing it with the boys in a garage down three lanes until sundown. He despised studying and detested homework. Exams just weren't meant for him. Above all, he had fallen in love. Jake Ashton had seen the face of his soul mate in Emmy.

He never noticed how fast everything around was slipping out of his reach, and kept dreaming, until one day when he could not contain it any longer, he decided to speak to the grown-ups about a wedding; perhaps in a couple more years. For him the very next moment was perfect, he thought with a smile. He would abduct the parish minister; get them bound in holy matrimony and race with Emmy all the way to the other end of the world if he could.

When Jake reached home that evening, the Sparks had been invited over for tea. His smile widened when he caught a glimpse of Emmy in a corner, sipping quietly. Jake had entered whistling a happy tune, and decided right away that any time was the best time to propose a wedding; a big white one with a marquee in the backyard, children running around, the smell of delicious food, and music, yes; the band would play finally after all the practice he had got from ditching those boring classes.

He would sing for her on their wedding, how lovely! Definitely no kidnapping ministers, that wouldn't be nice. The moment he let himself in, Mr. Ashton stepped before him. "You've been lying to us, son," he said softly, holding a sheaf of papers. Jake was still among the clouds, wondering what flowers should fill the backyard. They would have to bring in some good men to begin shaping the grass if it were to grow out in time.

"How could you do this to us? You've created such a big mess! What were you doing away from school? You're into drugs aren't you, you little-"

Jake wasn't taking in a single word his mother was aiming at him. "I want to marry Emmy," he blurted out. Instantly the entire scene seemed to freeze. Moments passed in shocked silence as shoulders stiffened all around. He had no clue what his crime was.

Emmy's mum stood up and the chair toppled over. A resounding crash cleaved the silence like a knife through warm butter. "Why!" she yelled, why would she ever let her daughter be married to a miserable little excuse for a young boy who had just got himself dismissed from school on account of prolonged absence without reason, failure to respond to previous warnings, multiple failures in every possible course, insufficient grounds for promotion, and possible drug abuse and antisocial indulgence during the aforementioned absence?

What had he been thinking, daring to ask for her daughters hand when they were both barely seventeen years of age, when he wasn't capable of even keeping himself at school? What were the Ashtons telling the children these days, she spat at Jake's parents, who remained silent.

"Mum, please," Emmy defended Jake with everything she had. Slap! Mrs. Sparks' hand fell across her daughter's soft cheek and it burned pink. Mr. Sparks picked up his glasses and walked out wiping them, having had enough. After this, Emmy heard the Ashtons had moved Jake to America, and she never heard from him ever again.

Years later when Andrew McFarland walked into her life, everybody thought that he was a fine young man. He had a steady job in an MNC in Tokyo that was gifting him a transfer, so he was coming to Lancashire to live with his mum. Mrs. McFarland adored the Sparks; they had met through overlapping social circles.

Emmy's heart had healed fast and her finger now ached for the ring. She didn't feel anything spectacular until she laid her eyes on Andrew on the day of their wedding. Then she knew she was in love. She loved Andrew in a way she had never loved anybody her entire life.

In the beginning, of course life was blissful. One day he came home and argued with her that the curtains in the living room were too dark. And then the couches were ugly the next day, and on the next the soup was cold. Soon Andrew raised his voice for no reason bigger than the most trivial things, and later in bed, he would reason with her blaming it on his work pressure.

"The Japs push me pretty hard in there," he would say, and Emmy would smile with calm understanding. She loved him with every sense, every cell, every breath she took, and every beat of blood in her veins. It shocked her when he pleased women at parties, ignoring her as if to disown her. Andrew would get drunk a lot more than often, and she would take off his filthy clothes and shoes, she would wash him, and tuck him into bed before mopping up the puke.

Emmy would never forget the day he had first hit her, hard across her face. Her eyes filled up with tears and Andrew saw them. Instantly something stirred him back to his senses, and he cupped her face in his hands. "I'm… I'm sorry, Emmy," he said.

And he was sorry. She knew, because she was in love with him.

Emmy hadn't been planning for motherhood anytime soon, but when it surprised her, she welcomed it. She was going to have a little Andrew or a little Emmy in nine magical months of cramps and morning sickness, and she embraced it.

One day Emmy was switching channels idly when something caught her attention. A new musician was born that season, his hit single soaring on all major charts, his albums selling tremendously after worldwide release. He was now touring Europe.

Andrew had, of course, known about Jake. Emmy's childhood friend, high school sweet heart. Dropped out, ran away to America. Unheard of since.

But that day he had stormed inside and banged the door shut behind him locking himself in without a word to Emmy. After around three hours of no response, Emmy heard the click of a lock, so she pushed open the door gently and approached him. Emmy's hands shook, but she gulped back her fears and placed a hand on his shoulder.

To her surprise, Andrew turned back and crumpled into her arms, terribly upset. He had been fired from his job, she learned, and Emmy's heart leapt out to him as she held him with gentle firmness, stroking his forehead, consoling him, telling him that she loved him. Perhaps they were bonding at last, she believed.

Meanwhile, Jake Ashton's tour had reached England, and the first face he wanted to see was Emmy's. He had heard that she was married, but he still cared for her. He wanted to wish her well and congratulate the lucky bastard McFarland.

Jake found Emmy's new home and when he visited she was pleasantly surprised, even mildly shocked that he had remembered at all. After all, he had never written even a postcard to her since he had left. This was when Jake and Emmy realized how their parents had intercepted all the letters they'd written until they simply lost hope and quit writing.

They talked about everything they had missed out on each other's lives, and how much each had changed. Jake had changed little; he still had the same boyish charm. Emmy had grown into a beautiful woman with a powerful gaze, hardened by experience yet mellowed by emotion when it called.

When Andrew walked in, despite being tired from the three interviews he had given just that day, he'd smiled at Jake. Introductions were made, and in the end as Jake walked away, he realized he was still in love, but felt a warm glow in his chest in knowing that Emmy was a happy woman expecting a baby.

The pressure from hunting for jobs was taking its toll on Andrew, and the news that Jake Ashton was delaying his European tour in England by a few weeks simply did not help. Jake kept visiting, showing no more than a friend's care, and often spending more time with Andrew than with Emmy. He was content with watching her happiness. Emmy was blissfully unaware of the clouds gathering fast, because she was desperately in love with Andrew.

The bad days came back when Andrew could not control his temper, and he slapped her every day. He demanded to know why Jake kept coming back, and what mattered more to her, her pathetic unemployed husband, or the rock-star who had just walked out of a movie with his perfect life. Andrew felt inferior, and that enraged him. The arguments never ceased, and the bruises on her face and neck were unanswered for.

The final fatal blow came when Jake visited Emmy for the last time to tell her that he was leaving. He had been told that Andrew was giving Emmy a hard time and she refused to blame him for anything. She was forever defending Andrew because she loved him with the last trace of her existence. But she was beginning to lose hope, she was growing weary. She was being hurt beyond measure and reason by the person she was desperately in love with. And nobody knew.

That day Jake stood outside on her doorstep determined to tell her he was leaving, continuing on his tour hoping that would help everyone. He rang the doorbell repeatedly, angry that Emmy was still in love, angry that she hadn't left the bastard.

After quite some time Emmy answered, with the same warm smile that had never left her beautiful face in all the years that had flowed in between them. "I'm leaving, Emmy," he said softly, and comprehension dawned on her face, and she nodded. There was sadness in her smile now, and Jake could not bear to have it there.

Before he knew what he was doing, he had lifted his fingers to brush across her soft cheek, the very same cheek he had kissed countless times in his dreams when he had been kept away. There was a purple bruise on her neck, and she flinched when his fingers brushed against it. Jake was beginning to say something, when his gaze fell behind her.

Jake felt ice in his chest as he saw the horror right before him. There was a small trail of dark blood from somewhere behind her on the white floor, ending in a little pool at her feet, staining her toes. A million horrible images flooded Jake's vision, of Andrew hitting her, the bruises, perhaps he had delivered a blow on her stomach which wasn't very big from the baby yet, a rush of images, which cleared as it hit him. The baby. He reached out to support Emmy as she collapsed onto his chest. "I love him, Jake," she whispered, blacking out.

* *

Emmy Sparks had no idea what she was doing here. She blinked in the colored lights dancing across the audience, a little sea of faces watching her, cheering for her. When she began to sing, the crowd was silenced instantly, the stadium was so quite you could hear a pin fall. She was fascinated by the way her voice bounced around, clear. Beautiful.

The words were pouring out from somewhere within her, bringing back something that had died long ago. In the crowd she could see Jake Ashton bringing in her parents and his, and there were faces she recognized here and there. The Sparks and the Ashtons were watching her, listening to everything that life had brought to her.

Every time she had listened to their choices quietly, asking for none of hers. Every moment spent with Andrew. Every time she had gently smoothed out the creases on his forehead. Every kiss, every touch, every glance, and every memory they had made together. The baby they would have made. The agony that had ripped her and sapped her strength, the anger at herself for being in love. The pain that shot through her nerves, the fear that crippled her will. The defiant silence that she had answered life with.

And yet, the courage that came only from love.

She sang, one after the other, every song born from all the words she had never once spoken, from all the pain she had let herself live through. From all the love she had been blinded by.

When the music ended, she watched the stadium explode in thunderous applause, and she saw Jake Ashton give her the thumbs-up with pride, and she saw the guilt in the faces of the grown-ups. So they knew, finally, they knew.

She was gulping down water and removing her minimal make-up after the concert when one of her very timid violinists entered the room and slipped her a small piece of paper. On it was a note scrawled in a very familiar writing of Andrew McFarland, and tears filled her eyes as a rush of memories came back.

He had been there, somewhere in the crowd, watching her.

Emmy,

You were amazing back there.

It's too late to say any more, but like you always wanted, I'm going to see a therapist. I'm going back to Lancashire, Emmy. Mum says she's baking muffins. I'll miss us eating them together.

I've always loved you. Always will.

Andrew

Emmy Sparks smiled as a fresh tear landed on the paper where he'd signed his name, and she breathed a prayer for him, content in knowing that he would be happy soon.

THE END

10. ANAYA

'Anaya' meant 'look up to God' in eastern Nigerian. She was dark, with high cheek bones, and deep-set dark eyes. She had Africa's magic in her, and everything around her thrived in that magic. She had in her the life and soul of that large black continent. Now around her the night was spreading quickly, and every time the spears clashed and the arrows flew past, the forest echoed with the noise. The clans were at war with each other all the time. But none had been this fierce before. Anaya slowly made her way deeper into the forest.

She was as agile as a mountain goat and quickly crossed over fallen logs and branches, and when she could no longer hear the screams of women and children and the war cries she sat down on the dark earth. She closed her eyes and leaned against the bark of a tree, drawing in a deep breath, taking in the scent of the earth, the breath of Africa.

As she sat, she brooded over the happenings. Men around her were fighting like savage beasts, killing and destroying mercilessly. Anaya let out a sigh. She looked up at the dark heavens, lit up with sparkling stars and a brilliant moon.

Suddenly, she heard footsteps. They were unfamiliar footsteps, not the kind that Anaya had ever heard in her life. She looked around, hand clasped around a knife hanging from her waist. She stood up and cried, "Simama!" (Stop!) drawing her knife. A group of men and women came out from behind a clump of bushes and scanned her cautiously.

Though Anaya did not realize it, they were a team from the United Nations, who had been sent to try and stop the tribal riots going on in those parts. The wars were really fierce, and they wanted to rescue and administer first-aid to women, children, the old and the sick, and stop the young chiefs from warring somehow. They stood looking at each other wondering what to do. One of them, a young white woman, took a step closer to Anaya and declared in pure Swahili, "Rafiki!" meaning 'friend'.

Anaya looked up at the heavens again, and belting her knife back to her waist, she let the woman lead her out of the forest.

* *

She was fed, warmed and taught. The UN team spent months counseling the clan chiefs and treating the sick and wounded, and during this time, Anaya learned more and more. She was taught to read and write in English, and she picked up quickly. She had in her a hunger to learn and know. When she heard that the UN team was going to travel further to Sudan, Ethiopia and Somalia she was excited and pled to be taken along. By then the peacekeepers had come to understand Anaya, and they took her along.

When Anaya stepped on the soil of Sudan one morning, she was excited. For her the world had been nothing more than her tribe and the neighboring tribes. Marian, the white woman who had spoken to Anaya in Swahili in the forest, had told her that the world was bigger than her tribe, it was bigger than Africa. She was now going to see a part of that world, and she was excited. Marian and the rest of the team were unloading hundreds of large crates of food and clothing from the trucks and Anaya helped.

She hopped about among the crates, wondering who wanted so much of food. She came from a tribe that had enough for themselves, and though she lived in Africa, she did not know what was happening all over it. She did not know that the magic of Africa was fading away fast to be replaced by poverty, war, AIDS and hunger. She picked up a bundle of blankets and followed Marian to what looked like a temporary house of some sort. It was a food camp organized by the UN. As she neared the camp, she realized something: there was a lot of noise around that house. They turned around the house-like structure, and the image flooded her eyes, and it dawned on her. She felt as though she had been struck.

All around, hundreds of children were crying, lying down or running around. Women were cradling infants, looking longingly at the crates of food. Anaya took a closer look at the people gathered, and a sharp pain seared its way through her heart. The children, even newborn babies, were nothing more than little black skeletons. Their faces and bodies were dusty and their lips were parched. Not a single child was smiling or laughing. But hundreds, she knew, were crying. As soon as they caught sight of the UN team, children crowded around, pushing and pulling, trying to get at the food in the crates.

"Here, Anaya, give these around," Marian handed a few packets of food to Anaya, who was standing as still as death. She took the packets silently and began handing them out to women and children. A little boy edged shyly towards her, and as she surveyed him, she noticed his skin clinging to his bones, the hunger in his eyes, and his tattered clothes. She bent down, handed him some food, smiled and asked him what his name was. "Jina lako nani?" she asked him. He gave an excited squeal and ran to hide behind his mother.

She continued handing the packets around, and an old woman, as she gratefully received her share, clasped Anaya's hand with her own skinny shivering fingers. "Mungubariki!" the old woman cried. ("God bless!") Tears stung Anaya's deep black eyes. She turned her eyes away from the sad, hungry crowd, and looked up at the heavens. She could not believe that this was happening.

"I have been blind," she thought. Marian was right. Africa was big, and the world was big. There was more hunger in this world than Anaya had ever imagined. After the food had been distributed, a video was shown to the children, and they cheered and shouted happily. The UN officials played games with them and distributed gifts and sweets. Then they were taken to bed, and Anaya watched a mother patting her child's stomach, sighing. It had been filled today.

That night, as she curled up in her sleeping bag, Anaya heard the cries of the hungry children repeatedly, and the pain shot through her nerves each time. She sobbed silently, thinking of the ocean of hunger she had seen that day. Their innocence, marred by poverty and hunger, tugged at her heartstrings. Her heart bled for them, for Africa, for the world. She tossed and turned, the shock of what had been revealed to her that day never fading.

Anaya sat up, running her long dark fingers through her hair. She got up and walked towards the children, sleeping peacefully, clinging close to their mothers. Tears leaked out of the corner of her eyes as she watched them. She stopped when she saw a little girl smiling to herself in her sleep, a hand on her tummy.

She looked up at the heavens again and back at the sleeping child. Here, in the heart of each child, lay the soul of Africa, she knew. In the smile of each of these children, lay the magic of tomorrow. As a large teardrop landed on the dark soil, Anaya looked up at God and resolved. "One day, Africa will smile," she whispered to the night.

THE END

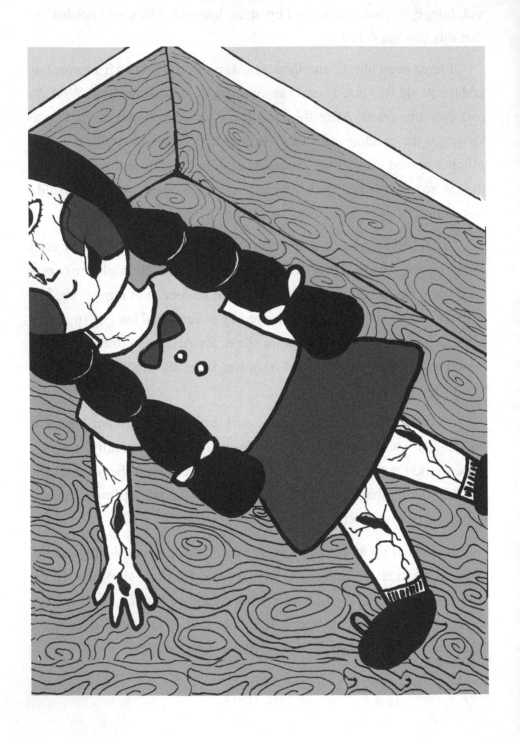

11. BLACK AND WHITE

The little girl's frightened screams echoed everywhere. She wanted to go out to play. Her aunt and uncle barely looked at her anymore. It was all a horrible dream ...they had locked her away. She'd never forget the tight cords they had bound her with, cutting into her skin...

Ethan Pierce opened the window and took a deep breath. It was a beautiful crisp morning. As normal as things could ever be. The night before, he'd taken Ruth out to dinner and they'd had a great time together after ages. Sure, she thought he was a workaholic, but after yesterday she had to have thought otherwise. He was a dentist, and off lately he'd been busier than usual. Ethan sighed happily.

"Ethan!"

He turned. Ruth was sitting up on the bed, feeling about her ankle. She had a strange look on her face. "Ethan. Get rid of these." She said, still smiling in that same strange way. Ethan looked at her ankles. There was nothing there. He walked toward the bed and sat on its edge, placing his hand on Ruth's ankle. "What's happening? Does it hurt?"

For a fleeting moment, he thought he saw something cross her face. But then she was relaxing again. She pushed his hand away playfully and laughed. "Of course it doesn't hurt. So, Mr. I've-no-idea-what-a-workaholic-is, what's the plan today?"

Ethan grinned. "I'm fixing breakfast."

Ruth put on a horrified look. "No way! You're a disaster! You can't cook."

He threw back his head and laughed.

They had a great morning and Ethan soon left for work. Ruth sat back leafing through a magazine. The T.V. was switched on, and she glanced callously at it now and then, sipping a cup of tea.

She listened to the key sliding into the hole. They were coming back! Maybe they were sorry. Then everything would be okay. Maybe they'd buy her a new doll! She remembered how her china doll's perfect face had been shattered. She'd never forget how that had hurt her.

Ruth was staring at something in the magazine. It was a piece on abused children. There was a little boy who'd been repeatedly beaten by his baby sitter. Somewhere in her head, she could hear the phone ringing shrilly. She took no notice.

There was something about a girl who'd been mistreated by her neighbor. Maybe Ethan was ringing to ask if things were fine. Why would they not be fine? There was a landlord who'd threatened to kill a tenant's children because he failed to pay rents.

The ringing turned into screams in her head.

Her uncle slapped her. She was shocked and angry. He said she was too expensive to look after.

The door creaked open and her aunt stood in the doorway, her face half obscured by the dark. She bent down and slid a small tray towards her. The little girl crawled eagerly toward the tray and began eating. The food tasted horrible...a stench hung about the bread...

Ruth stared hard at the glossy page. Stale food. They'd given her stale food.

She scanned the pages. At the end of it, something caught her eye. She was breathing very hard now.

'If you hear strange noises from next door, or notice a change in your child's behavior, please contact us immediately. At any hour, do not hesitate to place a call in the toll free child help line number. Are you a child in distress? Get help. Now.'

God, it hurts so much...nobody can hear me crying. Who will I ask for help?

She dialed the child help line number and listened eagerly. "Hello?"

* *

Ethan was examining an infected molar when the phone call was put through to him.

"Hello, Ethan Pierce. Who's calling?" "Boston Police, sir." Ethan was taken aback. "Oh. What can I do for you?"

When he reached the hospital, an officer explained to him that a hysteric woman had contacted child help line and given an address somewhere in Canton. When the police reached the address, they found that nobody had lived there for years. So they traced the phone call, and it took them to Ethan's house. They took the door down, and found Ruth cowering under the dining table, nearly faint with fear.

Ethan listened in shocked silence as the officer finished speaking, expecting him to react. When he said nothing, he was taken to Ruth, who was being examined. The psychiatrist smiled calmly when Ethan entered the room, and instantly he felt himself relax. Instead of talking to Ethan, the doctor was already speaking to the seemingly unconscious Ruth. "What's your name, dear?"

"Logan. Ruth Logan."

"How old are you Ruth?"

"Eleven."

Ethan felt a chill go down his spine as he listened to a little girl speak through his wife.

"Are you hurt, Ruth?" The doctor continued.

"Yes. Yes, it hurts."

"Can you tell me what happened?"

Ruth described how her mother had moved out when she was little, and when her father passed away, his cousin's family had taken her in. How they had begun to resent her and found her a financial burden as she grew up, and how they began mistreating her. How she was beaten, and locked up. How she was offered stale food. How they'd broken her beautiful china doll, how they'd trampled all over her childhood. How they'd blacked out all the color in her little world.

"Ruth. Do you know who I am?" The psychiatrist finally asked her after listening patiently. She replied that she didn't.

"I am a doctor, Ruth. I'll make your pain go away. Will you let me?"

"Okay. I think I like you."

"I'm glad you do. Now you can go to sleep. When you wake up, there will be no pain anymore."

"Doctor? Will you- can you fix my doll? I- I really like her."

Hot tears slithered down Ethan's face. Even the psychiatrist was hesitant. "When you wake up, everything will be fixed."

* *

Ruth was lying on the hospital bed. She looked very different to Ethan, but the doctors wanted to make sure they'd done their best. Once again, she was seemingly asleep.

"Can you tell me your name, dear?" The psychiatrist asked her.

"Ruth Pierce."

"How old are you?"

"I'm twenty five."

"How do you feel, Ruth?"

"Good. I'm fine."

"Do you think you were sick?"

"Maybe. I- I think so."

"Okay Ruth." He paused, choosing his words carefully. "Do you remember a doll you had, which you really liked?"

Everyone waited anxiously for Ruth's answer.

"Yes." Ethan could almost feel his heart sinking. He felt everybody in the room stiffening.

The doctor took a deep breath. "Do you remember what happened to her?"

"Yes. She was destroyed by my relative. We had a spot of trouble."

"Is that all?" The doctor was almost incredulous.

"Yes. That's all."

The doctors and nurses smiled at Ethan. Somebody showed a thumbs-up sign. He went down on his knees before them, sobbing in relief.

* *

"Hurry up, Ethan! We have to get something nice for Megan's little girl." A couple of months later, Ruth and Ethan were entering a store to buy a gift for their neighbor's daughter, who was having a birthday party.

There were so many toys, teddy bears and dolls. Ruth was already looking at a box of finger puppets when Ethan came up behind her. She put the box down, and slowly reached towards something on the shop window. Ethan followed her gaze to the picture perfect face of a pretty china doll. He froze, and looked at her, forgetting to breathe.

"Nice doll," she said, smiling and withdrawing her hand. Then she moved on. Ethan sighed in relief. "Yeah. Pretty."

THE END

12. SONGBIRDS

Molly Webster looked up at the tall gates, beyond which lay, what would be their new home. Beside her, she could feel Adam Webster's old hand tighten around hers. They had been married for a long time now. In that marriage their sons Peter and Mathew had blossomed, but Mathew had died a year ago. When a cancerous growth in the colon snatched their beloved son from them, Molly and Adam had leaned on Peter's firm shoulder. But Peter had decided their fate for them. He had brought them to these big iron gates, and now their destiny lay here.

Molly sighed, and together they stepped in. They were shown into their little room, and Molly helped Adam settle down. He sat staring through the window, rubbing his legs. An old happy tune played over his lips. Molly smiled, and she too leaned against him looking out of the window. "Here comes Christmas, and lots of white snow, here comes the winter, so cold and slow!" Adam whispered.

She placed a hand that was soft with age on his withered one. They sat together, reflecting old times. "Peter had loved having snowball fights with his friends during Christmas, but Mathew would shy away and help me in the kitchen. He would watch me prepare the candy canes, his eyes wide with fascination," said Molly.

They were lively, healthy children, and Molly was a happy woman. They had never expected events to take such a wild turn… but now they were here. Molly and Adam had each other…they would not be alone. They were candles in the wind…they would burn on till the end, bright as ever.

The morning wore on silently, though uneventful, it was damp with memories for the two of them. There were many old people like them here. There was good food, a warm bed to snuggle into at night. Molly sighed again. In the evening she held Adam's hand and walked around the garden and plucked a rose for him. He smelled it once, and they walked on. The home had a small chapel behind, where they lit two candles.

They had nothing left to pray for, no more dreams in life. So they simply stood and watched silently as the candles burned. Wax melted and piled slowly on the candle holders. Molly was reminded of the cozy evenings they had shared over the years, sitting huddled in front of a merry fire, munching happily on roast chestnuts and marshmallows.

Adam would tell the boys stories, and they would listen, watching the snow pile outside through the window. How long they stood watching the candles they did not know, but as they walked back to their room, the sun was retiring, with a promise to be back tomorrow.

They ate their dinner solemnly, and as they sat back on the bed, a tear trickled down Molly's cheeks as she remembered how the boys were tucked into bed with a goodnight kiss every night. Adam smiled sadly and wiped the tear away. Another followed it, and soon she was sobbing onto his sweater. Adam patted his wife. "There are no wounds that time cannot heal", he whispered. Molly rose and nodded, wiping her tear-streaked face with a handkerchief. "Yes," she replied. Time would heal.

Their days continued in this manner, and they accepted it. Adam and Molly never expected Peter to turn up at the gates with a bouquet of flowers and a big smile, waiting to take them back. It was too lovely a dream, it would never happen. They continued their walks to the chapel, where they lit candles and watched them burn.

Having each other to lean on, they decided that would hold on tight till the end. Peter never called, and they never expected him to. Life had gifted them with a happy marriage, healthy children, and many years of bliss. What more could they ask for? Now Peter had chosen his life, he had moved on. He was grown up; he had grown too big to fit in their hearts. But they had each other. Nothing mattered more than that. They had each other to hold on to and that was all that mattered.

Time flew by, and days became weeks, months and neared a year. On the eighteenth day of November, Molly and Adam stood before the chapel doors as usual. But today the candles would be brighter than usual; it was their wedding anniversary.

Molly thought of the two of them, young and thriving, walking down the church aisle hand in hand amidst cheer. She smiled and they lit yet another pair of candles, and stood back to watch.

Time has healed, she thought. She had never cried after that day. Though the boys' faces were forever etched on the walls of her shriveled heart, she shrank back from thinking of them. "Why must I?" she would say to herself.

She hoped that Peter's children would never do this to him. If they did, he would die a broken hearted man. Over the months Adam and Molly endured the pain together.

Another couple of months passed by, and one evening, after returning from the chapel, Adam sat rubbing his chest and humming an old tune. Molly smiled and settled beside him.

"A thousand lonely nights may pass...For me there is the moon and the stars..." he hummed an old tune. She hummed along, looking out at the starry sky. Their eyes met each other's and filled with tears. Through those tears, they sang together.

"A thousand lonely nights may pass...
For me there is the moon and the stars...
Now the sun may go...
It'll be back tomorrow...
If I had wings I'd fly away...
So much pain day after day...
Now you've left me alone...
I wonder if your heart is stone...
All I have for you is love...
Even as I leave for the heavens above..."

They sang till Adam lay back on the bed, and Molly rested her head on his chest. They sang for as long as they could through tears, and the last Molly felt was Adam's chest rising and falling slowly before she fell asleep.

As dawn broke, little drops of dew clung to the petals of the flowers in the garden and somewhere, hundreds of birds broke into song. It was a lament for the loss, a wordless song for the deceased. The cleaning lady found an old man and his wife in one of the rooms, still, pale and cold as death. Together they lay, hand in hand, hearts leaden with unspoken sorrow.

*   *

In a Home for the old, death was not something to be alarmed at, and the lady was used to this. Records called them Adam and Molly Webster. Their son was informed. By noon Peter and Francesca Webster arrived at the gates before which Molly and Adam had stood a year ago. Francesca was five months pregnant and in a terrible temper, so she chose to sit down in one of the plush chairs in the waiting room and rifle through a magazine.

Peter was shown into the room where the old couple lay- his parents. He looked at them once, and touched their hands, which were locked together. There was nothing more to be said or done. They were put to rest beside each other in the Home's own graveyard.

As Peter Webster backed his car out through the gates, the songbirds continued grieving.

THE END

13. SOMEONE

She sat on a bench at the station, clutching her coat tightly around herself, each breath let out forming a misty cloud before her. The cold was biting, her fingers were numb. She took out his letter and read it again, somehow willing it to ward off the cold wind. It said he'd come, that very day.

Two long and hard years had flowed in between them, each of which they had lived in moments. She wondered whether he looked any different now. Perhaps he had grown a beard? The letter said nothing about a beard. It did not matter. She blushed in the cruel winter's evening, the color barely visible. He would come, and soon, she thought.

"Will you have some coffee, miss-?" The voice startled her, and looked up to see the kind face of a man, with a smile that was warm despite the weather. He held open a flask and a couple of paper cups. "I-oh yes, I think I will," she said. He poured a steaming cup of coffee for her, and then one for himself. He then sat down beside her.

"Who's coming, then?" He asked her, gently sipping.

She took a sip of hers, and the warmth in her throat felt like it had come all the way from heaven.

"It's my husband."

He fell silent for some time.

"Have you waited long for this day?" He asked suddenly.

She nodded.

"Then the cold shouldn't matter."

She said nothing.

"Sometimes," he continued, "when you're waiting for someone you love, nothing matters. The cold doesn't get you. Heck, the devil wouldn't get you if he tried."

She smiled, nodding.

They looked up; they had heard a distant rumble on the rails. The people who had sat down jerked up and began pacing the platform immediately.

"What do you think; is he in that one?" He shouted over the noise as the train pulled in before them, huffing and puffing like an old man.

"Can't say, maybe," she shouted back.

Passengers piled out of the train, into the arms of eager families. Some sat back, disappointed, finding that their loved one had not been in that train. She scanned the thinning crowd; he would come by the next one. Silence settled in once more.

"I think I'll have another cup," the kind man said, holding up the flask expectantly.

"I think I will, too," she said.

"The name's Andrew, by the way," he told her as he poured.

"I'm Rosa," she paused, took a sip and then went on. "You're here for someone?"

"I'm meeting someone in the city," he paused and then asked quietly, "Ever wondered what it's like to have no one to wait for?"

She looked at him. The smile was still there, as genuine as ever. She did not know what to say. "Not really." She heard a sigh escape him.

"Well, it isn't pleasant."

"I- I'm sorry," Rosa responded, not knowing what to say.

"Oh that's alright. It's just that," he lifted the flask of coffee, "sometimes, life is like this flask of drink…and you've got to have it all alone. And that's no fun."

She couldn't help but smile. "So fill two cups. Find someone to have the other one," she shrugged.

He smiled too. "Don't I look a wee bit too old for that?"

"Absolutely not," she said indignantly, and he chuckled softly.

"Tell me about your husband." He sipped.

"Well, we've been married for two years. James left a week after our marriage, to the army. He's coming tonight, and he's going to stay. He's a great person- kind, caring, considerate, humorous, and decisive but not imposing, fun to be with- everything I could ever ask for."

"Sounds like you're in love," he winked.

"I am," she winked back.

"It is great being in love, isn't it?" Andrew asked her. She looked down. "Indeed, it is," Rosa whispered, thinking of James longingly.

* *

The man sat back, watching the mist condensing on the window. Two years, he thought. It's been so long. How much had she changed? Or had she at all? It did not matter. He would be with her soon. He looked at his watch impatiently. "Nearly there," somebody said. He looked up, to see a beautiful woman smiling at him, sitting directly opposite him.

She had perhaps been watching him for some time. He smiled back. "Who's waiting for you?" She asked him. "My wife," he said, beaming.

"Has it been long?"

He nodded vigorously. "It's been two years."

The woman held out a box of chocolate. "Here," she said. "I'm Helena," She told him. "I'm James," he said, accepting a piece from the box.

"It's wonderful having someone to wait for you, isn't it?" she said, looking out through the window as the train pulled to a stop.

James nodded, thinking of Rosa; she would be at the next station, waiting for him.

"I should say it is. And this is delicious by the way," James said. "Please have some more. It's just the way life is. We have to keep it sweet…or it tends to turn sour," Helena responded smiling.

James nodded, and not knowing what to say, he asked, "So you have something to do in the city?"

"I'm meeting someone."

"So what's your wife like?" The woman asked him. He was only too glad to reply. "My Rosa's a wonderful woman. I had to leave her a week after we got married, and that was the toughest thing I've had to do in life. But that's how being in the army is, though, most of the time. Rosa knew that when she married me. She's an angel, I'll say. She's a real angel."

He tossed the colored wrappers out through the window, and as the train picked up speed they watched little pieces of color fly around. "Ever wondered what it's like to have nobody to wait for you?" Helena asked suddenly. James shrugged. "Hmm…I don't really know how that's like," he told her.

"I'll tell you that it isn't pleasant…life's like those wrappers in the wind… a million little pieces…after everyone and everything's gone, they are left behind, fluttering aimlessly."

She let out a soft sigh. "Well, then let those torn wrappers go. Find new sweetness in life." He smiled. She did, too. "You think that'll happen?"

"Why shouldn't it?"

The train was halting again. Travel-worn passengers collected luggage and stepped out stretching, and eager families rushed forth to welcome their loved ones.

James emerged from the crowd on the cold platform, and he found a slim, dark haired woman walking towards him. "Rosa!" He said softly. She seemed to shiver with tremendous joy and in her eyes swirled a beautiful green sea of boundless love. "You're no different," she said. "Neither are you," he replied. "Why are we whispering?" she asked, ever so softly. He hugged her.

"We're just happy." They held hands all the way home, laughing and joking.

* *

Andrew crushed the empty cups. James was home, and Rosa was gone. He sighed, and got up to leave. There was a little shop near the station, where he bought flowers. He walked on, into a graveyard. The silence was sickening.

He stepped among grassy graves and headstones wet with fresh tears and rain. He stopped, bent and placed the flowers on one of them. On it was engraved, as was on his heart, "Cassandra Wagner- Forever Immortal." He had indeed been in love, once upon a time. Andrew's other cup belonged here, where forever it would.

* *

Helena parted the crowd and hailed a cab to the Cancer Centre in the city. Everyone there knew her, and she knew them. She turned the handle of a door to be warmly welcomed by a ten-year old boy. She unloaded chocolates onto the white hospital bed, listening to his gleeful exclamations.

He would be waiting for her this way, until death did them apart. Together, they would fight till the very end to keep life sweet.

* *

Everybody in the world has a different story to tell.

Everyone who's smiling at you today may have a raging ocean of sorrow in their hearts. The saleslady who packed your grocery, the postman who brought in the mail, the newsboy, the actor in the movie you watched yesterday, the comedian who cracked the joke over which you laughed last week, your manicurist, your dentist, your driver, the President, and just about everyone in the world have their own story.

Some are too proud to cry, some laugh through tears.

You meet so many people, some who mean so much to you and some whom you have no idea about. People come and go; some stay, yet many are forgotten.

We mourn for those who die; but we never even understand the agony that's alive in hearts around us.

You could be lonely in a crowd, smiling for others, burning up inside. You could love a million people; but if tonight is your last, you would never be able to let them know just how much you cared.

Look around you; perhaps, a stranger will smile.

THE END

Helena passed the result and pulled a cab to the Cancer Centre in the city. Everyone there knew her and she knew them. She turned the handle

Helena

14. SURVIVORS

You know, those times in life when you get into something and then wonder why you did it in the first place? Everybody faces a dilemma about career, relationships, and family at one time or the other. Ultimately, it's your choice...and the regrets are yours too. I'm Erica Thornton, a freshly baked bun straight from the oven, having completed a diploma in psychology.

I've recently joined training in the de-addiction centre in the Aid Medical Campus Hospital, which is pretty famous. When I first heard of Aid, I was really interested, and hoped to find myself working for it after the course. I thought de-addiction was definitely something new, something different. I chose it, and the regrets are solely, entirely, mine.

Every day, unhappy men and women, addicted to everything starting from alcohol right down to caffeine turn up in my clinic, wanting to trace back to where they began. I get paid for helping them out of the mess they've created. I began training here five days ago. There is so much of despair around this place, and I feel so horrible having to come here every day and work with these unhappy people. I'm still young, and I do have time to turn around from this depressing and hopeless environment.

I think the negativity of the whole thing might just make me quit any day now. Ah well, so what do we have today? My first meeting is with Morris Flake to tackle his chocolate problem. Kenneth Goodman comes next, a dedicated smoker. Amanda Ryan, unlisted...Excuse me? I have a patient, erm, client whose problem isn't mentioned. Amanda Ryan, complaint unlisted, is meeting me right after lunch. I decided to see to the matter later.

"Come on in, Morris! So how's it going eh?" I beamed at the man, giving him the brightest smile that was humanly possible. He sighed and sat down before me, and thus, another long, depressing day began.

* *

At lunch that day, my friend Lilly Sayer, who was an intern like me at the Aid Obesity Clinic, pointed out the mistake in my chart. "So what's Amanda Ryan doing here, unlisted?" she asked me. "I have no idea," I said, looking up from my salad. I had just another session, and then I was free, free from this damp, dreary place! I made a mental note of all the pleasant things I had to do, before I lost myself to the misery around the place.

Lilly finished eating, packed up, nodded at me and left. I cleared slowly, and set off to the de-addiction centre.

I pulled the door open, and found that the room was occupied already. I wondered, and stepped into view. "Um hello- Amanda Ryan?"

She was a tall brunette, with eyes and clothes the color of the darkest night of the year. She looked real scary to me. A fresh fact sheet had been placed on my desk with her name on it. When she spoke, her voice was firm. "Hello."

So what do I do, cheer? I have a murderous-looking woman with an affinity towards black sitting all alone with me, myself absolutely clueless about the whole thing. But I had to start it somewhere, and end it somewhere.

"So, how're you today Amanda! What can I help you with?" I tried to smile, but for some reason wondering when she was going to pull out the poisoned knife and drive it through my heart; which was, sadly then located in my throat.

Amanda surveyed me for a moment, and then took a long breath before she began. "I am an alcoholic." She paused. I waited, nodding.

"I drank regularly," Amanda continued, "in careful amounts, at parties, with friends, never too much or too little. Then I just kept at it. I loved how it made me feel. I thought that I had complete control of what I was doing. But then...I..." My expression softened. "Go on," I urged her gently. "But then I didn't know what I was doing," Amanda shook her head. "I drank, as usual, at a party one night...I didn't know it...but I was pregnant."

She got up and walked to the window, and for the first time, I noticed that somebody else had been in the room with us. A little boy with curly brown hair came back with her. Amanda was sobbing quietly now, and so would anyone, taking a look at the child. I understood the woman, and my heart bled for her. She had unknowingly destroyed the boy, and she lived on bearing the guilt and pain of what she had done.

"Nick is four," she said. "He cannot speak or understand us, but the doctors say...the doctors say..." She looked down, and I knew she was fighting bravely. "Sit down, Amanda," I told her. I walked around the table and picked the boy up, placing him on the desk. His eyes were glassy, and there was a charm about his little face.

Amanda had her head in her hands. "The doctors say..." she was mumbling. "And that's exactly where we start! We have the doctors Amanda, and we have to believe in them. Nick believes in you. He wants you to start hoping!" I said patting her. I consoled her, listened to her, and cheered her up, laughed with her and assured her that Nick's life could change. I referred her to a really good doctor at the clinic who could help

Nick. I suggested that she took up some hobby, and that she rediscovered herself.

That had been the longest session I had been through. I thought of all the unhappy men and women, some with bloodshot eyes, others with marks on their wrists, where needles had pierced them. I thought of the burden they shouldered, the guilt of having exposed their blood to poison...They weren't dead but not really living either. I thought of the countless times they must have wanted to quit life...to turn away...

With a shudder I realized that each of them had times in their life when they could have quit...but they had not. Instead, each and every one of them had decided to stay, fight and live on. That was why they were here...that was why I was here. I was here to remove the despair around them...to fight it beside them; to heal, and to be healed. The service I was being trained to do...to show them the way back...my very presence and effort...was hope.

I scheduled weekly sessions for Amanda and she never failed to visit me every week. She was undergoing a transformation- I could see it every meeting. I could see that it was difficult... more for her than others. Talking about what was happening to her was beginning to get easier... and it was going to help, I promised her.

At the end of six months, she looked beautiful, having switched to bright happy shades of clothes; she was taking care of her hair. She had begun listening to music, reading, cooking, gardening and more. Nick had begun treatment, and the doctor that I referred him to guaranteed improvement.

Amanda was happier. Things were turning around for her.

I had changed, too. I ordered fresh flowers for my office every day, got brighter curtains and wallpaper, set up a little candy-station in the lobby, and asked for cartoons to be played for kids in the waiting area and to turn it into a recreation room with games and books. I saw the fruit of this decision when I heard our resident marijuana addicts laughing their muddled heads off one evening. More than everything, the way I felt about addiction had changed.

As the end of my internship of a year approached, I was interviewed. "Why do you think people who have ruined themselves should be helped, Erica? Must they not bear the consequences of deliberate actions?" I smiled, remembering how I had asked myself this question. "Everyone must pay for their deeds. These people must pay too, and they have, with a good part of their own lives, sir. But I stand for their cause, because they have fought bravely the desire to quit, ending it somewhere once and for all. To survive, living through the pain, is much harder than quitting. They have fought bravely, and they are survivors."

I was handed a letter not only declaring that I had successfully completed my training, but offering me a job at Aid Medical Campus as well. At the get-together held for Aid Medical Campus staff, interns, patients and well-wishers, I sang the song I had written for those I had met and helped during my training. I saw that their bloodshot eyes and tattered hearts were beginning to clear, and they were beginning to dream. I sang to them, telling them never to let go.

"I have a song for those dying
But this one's for those surviving
If you close your eyes the pain may end
But you have dared to come this far

No, don't let go of life
Don't give up without a fight
Because you are here to survive
Just hold on tight

There are those times in life when you
Wonder if you should just go
Because it's easier that way
Because it takes much more to stay

But you can be your own hero
So don't let go
Feel the heat of the fire in you
And the beat of a lion's heart
So let's stay and face life
Let's smile and survive
Let's hold on tight...
I stood amidst thunderous applause and teary eyed smiles.

When Morris Flake got married at the age of 57, I popped chocolate into his mouth at the wedding. When Kenneth Goodman quit smoking and took up basketball, I was there to cheer for his first club match. Nick Ryan had improved with physiotherapy and more; he could now say few words, and had begun to smile often. Amanda's joy knew no bounds.

I took up the job in Aid, and was placed in charge of new interns, while I cared for my own patients. I wrote in medical journals, I gave speeches and sang in other hospitals and doctors' clubs. In December a year from then, Amanda and Nick visited me while I was decorating the hospital along with staff. I handed a box of candy cane to Nick and he smiled. Amanda held his hand, and they walked beside me while I helped put up more decorations here and there.

It was after some time that two little words fell out from Nicholas Ryan's mouth, which meant the world to me. "Thank- you." He pronounced it clearly and carefully, word by word. I bent down and hugged the little boy, and felt exhilarated. Tears stung my eyes- I let the joy seep into every corner of my mind.

Climbing uphill and reaching heights is one thing. Holding another's hand while doing so, is entirely different. That way, when you reach the top, you can always share the joy.

THE END

15. LIFE

When eleven year old Maurine France returned from school one afternoon, she found that her mother had come home early. She doesn't do that often, thought Maurine. She wasn't surprised to see Jenny in bed. "What's up?" she asked, dropping her bag at the foot of the bed. "I don't think I'm too well, dear. This terrible headache..." Jenny drifted off absent-mindedly.

Maurine had lost her father at the age of three, and you couldn't say she was really missing him. Frederick France, being an explorer, had been away from home almost all the time. So he hadn't much time to get close to Maurine. But Jenny still missed him very much.

Maurine didn't mind, actually. She was only 11, but she had all the experience to know that this was life. Sometimes we lost, sometimes we gained, and it was all part of the game.

"What do you mean?" Maurine raised an eyebrow. During the past few days, Jenny had been acting rather oddly. She had been restless, sometimes clutching her head, or sobbing silently. There was something terribly wrong with her.

One evening she had come home very late, and as Maurine always stayed alone after school, she wasn't scared. She wanted to know where her mother had been. But Jenny just mumbled something about doctors and headaches and painkillers and fell fast asleep on the couch.

Now she was shivering. "Tell me mom, what's wrong with you?" asked Maurine. But her mother just turned her head and bit the pillow.

"Go on," Maurine urged gently, fondling her mother's hair. It was hard to tell who the mother was now.

"Maurine, I just have a fever," Jenny said without meeting her daughter's eyes. She smiled weakly. "We have to go to the doc, mom. It isn't just a fever. I know, I just know," said Maurine.

Maurine went to the kitchen and set the kettle boiling for tea. She often made strong tea for Jenny and milky ones for herself. Maurine was sure that something was certainly wrong with her mom. She decided to force her mother to visit the doctor.

When she brought the tea tray to her mom, she found that Jenny couldn't even sit up properly. She was very weak. But she cheered up a bit after the tea. Maurine couldn't help smiling then, even after her worries about her mother's illness. Jenny always loved her daughter's strong teas. Maurine went to bed disturbed that night.

The next day was a holiday. Maurine woke up early. When Jenny woke up long afterwards Maurine forced her to get ready for the doctor. Jenny looked at Maurine. Then all of a sudden she wrapped her eleven year old daughter in a tight hug. "I love you ever so much," she whispered, as a tear fell from her tired eyes.

* *

Maurine held her mother's hand tightly in hers and entered the doctor's room. Dr. Belinda Peterson was an old friend of Jenny's.

"Good morning, Jenny. How do you feel now?" she asked, motioning for them to sit down. "No better, Linda. Only worse," Jenny described unhappily. The two friends talked as though they had met only yesterday.

"Dr. Peterson, it's alright. You can stop ignoring me and tell me what's wrong with mom," Maurine interrupted. "Maurine, you don't...? Jenny, let me do the talking now, dear," said the doctor. "Maurine, I expected this from you soon or later. Maybe you won't understand exactly what Jenny's got, not when even we, doctors, don't get it."

Jenny sobbed quietly while Dr. Peterson explained all about it. Maurine didn't quite understand everything, but she nodded when the doctor reached the part where her suspicions had been correct. It was not just fever, not cold. But something much more complicated.

"I do wish I didn't have to say this," continued the doctor. "But Jenny is in the last stage, and I really don't think she should run around with you any more, Maurine."

"Jenny," she said, removing her glasses. "You need rest, dear. My prayers will be with you."

Maurine was left on her own for sometime while the two friends hugged each other. She didn't know what to think. What could she do for her mother before she left this world?

They walked back home, Jenny occasionally wiping a tear. When they reached their apartment, they looked at each other for the first time since they left the hospital.

"Mom, what do you want to do? We'll do something special before... before you go," said Maurine. For an eleven year old girl who had just realized that her mother was going to die, Maurine was showing amazing courage. She could have simply burst into tears, and hugged her mother. But she knew that her mother had just a few days left, and she wanted them to be special.

The tears that welled inside Jenny's eyes had more love than anything. Her tear glands were working furiously, and she was doing nothing to control them. Maurine wanted to cry, too, but she fought with her emotions and locked them inside some faraway chamber of her mind.

Jenny hugged her daughter. "Oh Maurine, I'm ever so sorry I didn't tell you. I love you so much." The following days passed in silence. Jenny had always wanted to go to Frederick's old house, though she hadn't been allowed in, because of the row that had taken place after Frederick had married 'that orphan girl'.

Yes, Jenny was an orphan and had grown up in the Angels' Mother Orphanage near the King Solomon's church where she had first met the handsome youth- Frederick France, who had later become of the famous overseas explorers.

While Jenny visited the church, she told Maurine tales about her dad. For the first time in her life, Maurine missed her dad. She knew she would soon be missing her mom too.

Each day, before going to bed, the mother and daughter knelt down and prayed with torn hearts. And after each day, Maurine hoped against hope that a ray of light would pierce the darkness that covered their little world. But none came.

Dr. Belinda Peterson visited them many times and she joined in their prayers. She tried to convince Jenny to stay at the hospital, but Jenny would not listen. "I don't want to die on that white bed, Linda, with disease all around me and far from Maurine," she said. "I want to spend my last days with her, in my house." Jenny closed her eyes and held her friend's hand, perhaps for the last time.

Jenny's death had been silent, too. There had been no one to mourn for her, except Maurine, holding her hand. Jenny had been extremely ill that night. She had asked for the family photo on the mantelpiece, which she had kissed and held tightly in one hand. The she whispered to Maurine, "I'm not leaving you, Maurine. I will always be with you, and so will your father. God bless you my child. God bless you." And she died.

Just like that.

Suddenly, for the first time in her life, Maurine France felt lonely. She carefully set her mother's cold lifeless hand down. Then she broke into tears, after all these days. Her tears were not an answer to all the problems she was facing, but it was a relief for her to have her tear glands well and alive, after so many days of suppressed sorrow.

After some time, she tried to call Dr. Belinda Peterson, but apparently she was busy in the middle of an operation- a serious case of life and death. She wasn't available. Maurine hung up. She felt like a dry rose near a dead rose. And this was life.

* *

Life is much like a story. It goes on and on, endless, and when you're least expecting it, it takes a wild turn, and dash into death. It is challenging, yes, very much. Maurine's life had been her mother.

But that wild night, July 19, two years ago, when the storm had been raging outside, that life had ended. Just like that. This was a new life, another wild night, and here was Maurine, tired after having put the children to bed.

Dr. Peterson had offered to look after Maurine, but the young orphan had insisted on going to the Angel's Mother Orphanage, near the King Solomon's church, behind which Jenny France's grave lay, next to Frederick France's grave.

Jenny had taken Maurine's dreams and hopes along with her in death, but Maurine wasn't lonely in the orphanage. Orphans like her surrounded her. She was just another new bee in the happy, buzzing beehive.

She replaced the book she had been reading to the children on the bookshelf and went in to check whether all the children were properly in bed.

Yes, they were.

She went to the kitchen and made herself a cup of tea, strong this time, not milky, and settled down on the rocking chair by the window.

Maurine France looked out at the dark stormy night. She sighed and sipped her tea as another death anniversary of Jenny France passed silently.

A tear fell onto her lap.

This was life, she thought. Sometimes we lost, sometimes we gained, and it was all part of the game.

This was life.

THE END

16. DON'T!!!!!

Dear Mom, Dad, Jane, Dennis, Pam, Joe, Grandpa Alex, Grandma Polly, Grandpa Ted and Grandma Rose,

Phew! Finally I get to sit down somewhere and write to you. It's been one hell of a week, what with all we've got to study; we have projects and experiments too.

So how's it going everyone? How's Mick? Hope he hasn't bitten the postman again! The last time that happened, old Anderson had to breathe into a paper bag because Mick scared the sock off him. What's Jane up to these days? How's school, Pam? And Dennis, do you still keep those weird creepy crawlies? There are like a gazillion other things under the sun and you think of collecting those disgusting things! Keep them well away from Grandma Polly; you know how they drive her insane. If Joe hasn't already done that, that is. He's become quite a naughty little thing hasn't he? I remember how he dropped red ants into my pants last summer. Can you believe a whole year's gone by since then?

Dad, obviously you've lost the car keys by now and everyone's keeping quiet because I'll be mad, so the extras are in the bread box. If you lose those, which I know you will, I'll write to you where the others are. I'll be blessed if you haven't managed to lose your head anywhere!

Mom, the sweater you made is amazing! Looks like I got the wrong one though, because my name isn't Pam, I'm Peg, remember? But it's lovely anyway!

Jane, next time you bake those muffins, make sure you don't blow the house up. It's best if you don't enter the kitchen until you can move around without breaking half a dozen cups.

Dennis, keep Mick well away from the postman. We can't afford to have him tearing after the poor guy down the country. Don't forget to fix all the leaks before the place is flooded. Don't look at Dad – trust me, he wouldn't notice it if the house was floating.

Pam, get Joe the wooden truck he wanted for Christmas (break the piggy bank!). Do tell Joe he isn't supposed to be Super Mechanic Man if there's anyone like that and take off the wheels and all the screws because he isn't getting a new one soon. I doubt it'll last the whole year.

Joe, be a darling. I know the word's got nothing to do with you, but be as close to it as you can. Get apples and sugar for the pony.

Dad, take good care of the plants okay? Call Cousin Katie over if the saplings look sick. Call Uncle Monty over if the horses look sick. Call the doctor over if Grandpa Ted looks sick.

Mom, don't let Dad break a finger on another of his engineering sprees okay? Dad, don't laugh too hard – I know you're going to hang another picture on the wall and end up nailing yourself down. And don't-I mean DON'T – take the old car apart. It doesn't even remotely resemble a car anyway, after the last time you fiddles with it.

Grandpa Alex, I understand you were great with horses, but you're a century older now, remember? So do not try to ride Big Jeff, simply because he will knock you down before you can say 'I'm Alex Birmingham'.

Grandma Polly, since your husband is probably laughing his head off behind you, and will obviously try to ride Big Jeff, please remember: when you hear the crash, do not faint. It means that Grandpa Alex has broken his nose. It also means that he needs a doctor, and that he may not resemble your husband anymore.

Grandpa Ted, you see how your pal ends up breaking his nose being naughty, so you do not assist him in anymore of his ventures. Also, do not stick your hand in the cookie jar, because the last time you did that you couldn't pull it back out and then we had to break the jar and you weren't allowed cookie for a whole week, which, if you remember was highly unpleasant.

Grandma Rose, do not let your husband stick his hand in the cookie jar. Or worse, climb the roof to rescue the cat when it's stuck up there.

And DO NOT set the rat in the rat trap free. It's a rat, remember? It isn't doing any good to the world anyway. But it's doing considerable bad to us.

Say hello to Uncle Monty, Cousin Katie, the neighbors, the grocer, the postman, and everyone else you can get hold of. Jane, don't forget to lock in the horses, dogs, cats, hens, and Dad. Joe, do not stick your finger in the fishbowl, because obviously there is FISH in it.

Everyone, hold on until I get back in summer. And hello, I need the house upright when I come home. Keep the heads and limbs screwed tight on!

Lots of love,
Peggy

THE END